Pocket Aces
Ain't All That

A Poker Player's Nightmare

Hal Hankey

PublishAmerica
Baltimore

ISBN: 978-1-60749-700-4 (softcover)
ISBN: 978-1-4489-1108-0 (hardcover)
PUBLISHED BY PUBLISHAMERICA, LLLP
www.publishamerica.com
Baltimore

Printed in the United States of America

D edicated to my poker buddies and all those I've ever had the
pleasure of competing against, some whose first names may
or may not be mentioned in this book.

Pocket Aces Ain't All That

A Poker Player's Nightmare

Chapter One

Todd grew up learning the games of poker from his father and grandfather, both avid players. At the age of 13 he was already playing with adults that were well seasoned in all aspects of the game. At first either his father or grandfather would play in the same game but that soon came to a halt when the other players refused to show up. It was rumored that the three of them had certain signals they used to let the other two know their hand was the nuts. In order to keep the weekly games going, two of the three would sit out until their turn came up the following week.

Todd won a lot of money from the other seven players making him think he was a much better player than he actually was. Little did he realize he was playing with guys that were known in the local poker circuit as 'dead money'. A dead money player is one that is incapable of knowing the odds or percentages of having the better hand. He will call most any bet, chase possible straights or flushes, or think his small pair of fours is the best hand even if one or two players in front of him raises the bet.

The young man still had a lot to learn about the game but he would not find this out until he was up against seasoned cut-throat players that knew most everything in the book. Both father and grandfather failed him in this respect. It was not intentional on their part simply because they themselves never encountered the likes of professional players.

Todd continued his winning ways through high school sometimes winning up to two-hundred dollars per week. While in college he befriended classmates that played the game of 'Texas Hold-em', the game he loved the most. Unlike him, his college buddies all came from rich homes and it was nothing for them to get five hundred or more dollars per week allowance. Some had credit cards with a twenty thousand dollar credit line. Most of them received their allowances every two weeks and that is when the games were played. Todd, being more knowledgeable of the game, found himself winning constantly, sometimes up to four thousand dollars per month. He seemed to have more luck than he deserved.

The way they played 'Texas Hold-em' was turbo style meaning the forced bets, better known as the small and big blinds, increased every five to ten minutes. Each man was given one thousand five hundred dollars worth of chips. This does not mean that it cost each player that amount of money but in order to get that amount of chips to play with, each player would have to buy in for one hundred dollars. Each game consisted of ten players totaling one thousand actual dollars and the pay-out would be to the top three finishers, seven hundred to the last player remaining at the table with all the chips (first place), two hundred to the second place finisher and one hundred for the third place player. On a given night they could play up to four games. The eliminated players would often play side cash games until the tournament game ended and the next tournament started.

This one particular night was one of those that Todd could do no wrong. When ever possible he would limp in (meaning only having to call the big blind) with cards that any good player would normally fold then hit the flop big time (first three cards off the deck after the top card is discarded) for a straight, flush or set (set meaning three cards of the same rank). It was his night alright. He won three first places and one second for a total of twenty three hundred dollars. Not bad for a $300 investment.

By the time he graduated college he accumulated over twenty five thousand dollars that he kept in a small fire safe box hidden in the trunk of his old 1997 Chevrolet. He did this to avoid having to pay any taxes on it and to keep it a secret from his parents who, so graciously, paid his four year tuition.

He majored in business but was not about to go job hunting yet for he felt that he could possibly make it in the gaming field and become a professional poker player.

He dated a girl, named Debbie, while in college and planned to marry her as soon as he made his first million playing poker. On the day of their graduation he presented her with a diamond ring and promised to marry her as soon as he got back. Little did she know it was a ring he won in a poker game from a guy that owed him three hundred dollars. She accepted his proposal and promised to wait one year for him. If he did not return by then the engagement was off. With the blood of a gambler coursing through his veins he accepted the condition handed down to him and told her he would see her in one year.

Chapter Two

Before leaving for home he played one last game with the boys at the college dorm. During the game he found out from a few of them that their fathers knew of some games in Baltimore and Pittsburgh. Some of the players were district attorneys, police chiefs and entrepreneurs. They played cash games of Texas Hold-em and the buy in was normally ten thousand dollars. It was a fixed game with two hundred and four hundred dollar blinds and a maximum of three raises.

As he listened to all this, the adrenaline in his body began to rise. He rubbed his hands together like Tiny Tim did in the story of 'The Christmas Carol' when his father began carving the Christmas goose.

After the first game was over, which incidentally Todd won, he gave the two classmates his home phone number and asked them to phone him when they found out if it was alright for him to play in on of the high stakes game. It didn't matter what city he had to travel to.

He and his fiancée rode back home together. She lived in Harrisburg about twenty miles north of Todd's home. They went on several dates during the next three days and then the call came.

The message he got was, "If you got the ten grand your welcome to play." The game was scheduled for the following Wednesday in Baltimore at five in the evening.

Todd now knew it was time to level with his parents. They were unaware of the poker games he was involved in at college over the past four years. At first he thought it best to discuss this over dinner that very same night but decided against it. Knowing his father he was sure that he would tell him to go for it but his mother, a real conservative, would insist that he make a safe investment of his winnings and start getting some resumes' made up for distribution to various employment agencies. He decided to talk to his father first and then when he was well on his way to Baltimore his mother could be told the truth.

As Todd drove his car into his parents' driveway his father was just getting out of the family car. This seemed to be the golden opportunity he was looking for since the mother was in the house and unable to hear their conversation.

Todd jumped from his car and called out, "Dad, hold up a second, I need to talk to you without mom being around."

With a look of concern on his face the father replied, "Are you in some sort of trouble boy?"

Todd chuckled and said, "No dad, nothing like that. I'm leaving for Baltimore next Wednesday afternoon and I felt you should know why. I trust you not to say anything to mom what I'm about to tell you until I'm well on my way."

As the two walked up and down the driveway Todd told his father about the poker games and the twenty-five thousand dollars he won. As expected his father expressed pride as opposed to disappointment and gave his son a congratulatory pat on the back. "How can I be angry with a son that averaged six thousand two hundred and fifty dollars a year playing poker and graduate with a 3.2 GPA, you gotta love it!"

Todd was assured by his father that everything would be okay with his mother by the time he got home and not to worry about a thing. There was one condition, he had to take his cell phone along and keep his dad informed every chance he got.

There would be one more date with Debbie before he left and Todd wanted it to be a special one.

Knowing she loved stage performances, he bought tickets to the Harrisburg dinner theater club. The dinner was delicious and the play was very funny. It turned out to be a perfect evening for both. Caught up in the moment, he promised that if he won a large amount of money the first two things on the agenda was, first to find a good job and second to marry her sooner than they planned. The monies won would go toward the purchase of their own home.

Chapter Three

The following Wednesday Todd departed home around three in the afternoon, he wanted to be sure he found the Baltimore address on time. Like many other big time poker players, showing up late for a game was one of his superstitions and could make for a losing night.

Without any difficulty he found the address. Just as he was about to knock on the door a man from the street walked up to him and asked for his name. The man looked as though he could have been the police. With some hesitation Todd told him his name. He asked Todd if his car was locked and he told him it was.

Todd felt a little uneasy when he was asked to get in the late model black Cadillac parked across the street but with some reservation, did what was asked of him. As he got in the back seat he noticed there was another man seated in the front on the passenger side that also looked like a cop. As the Cadillac pulled away the man on the passenger side looked back at him and smiled, "All this appears somewhat like a cloak and dagger plot in the movies but we had to be sure we were picking up the right person. A year ago I was in a game when two guys came through the window in back of the building and took off with over ninety thousand dollars of our money, since then we are very secretive of the location of our games and we move it around the city from one location to another in order to avoid such a recurrence. My name is Tom and the guy driving is Scott, there's no need for last names. We're not hoods or criminals, just businessmen that love to play the game of Texas Hold-em. We avoid the big WSOP tournaments cause; quite frankly, they are a turkey shoot or lotto if you understand what I mean. We find it quite rewarding to sit at a table of eight or nine players that know how the game should be played."

Todd told Tom what he said made a lot of sense and he was looking forward to playing. Noticing that it was nearly five p.m. he mentioned the fact that he was superstitious about showing up late.

Both of the men chuckled and confessed that the game really started at seven. This was another of their precautionary moves to ensure the safety of the game when a new player is admitted.

With more than two hours left before game time they drove to the Inner Harbor for a bite to eat and a couple drinks.

After a few beers and a crab cake or two it was time to leave for the game. Todd was told he would be the youngest player at the table. The other players ranged from forty to sixty. For a guy of twenty-three he knew this might be somewhat intimidating, so it would be necessary for him to overcome this and play his game.

After approximately five or six minutes driving they pulled in front of large office building. They took the elevator up three flights and walked into a lawyer's office. The name on the door was O. B. Felix, criminal defense lawyer.

Todd was welcomed with handshakes and pats on the back. O. B. offered him a drink but rather than consume any hard stuff Todd chose a coke.

There were eight other players there and they were introduced by first name only. Besides himself there was Tom, Scott, O.B. (the only guy who's last name he really knew), Chris (who was referred all night as "The Master"), Daryl, Justin, Rick & Steve.

Chris was the banker and each gave him their ten thousand dollars. He carefully counted their money and in turn gave them that amount in chips.

When Todd took his seat he could not help but admire the poker table he bellied up to. It was first class in all respects and as good as or maybe better than some casinos. The felt on the table was exquisite and he couldn't help but run the tip of his fingers over it.

When everyone was seated the door to the room opened and in walked a lady dressed in a businessman's suit, necktie and all. She had to be between fifty and sixty years of age and quite attractive. With a smile she said, "Gentlemen, my name is Wendy, I'm your dealer for this evening. If anyone has a problem with that I will leave immediately without asking why. This is no limit Texas Hold-em and will be a cash game; the blinds will be fifty and one hundred dollars. Re-buys are permissible only after the chips in front of you are depleted; shall we get started?"

Wendy dealt one card to each in order to determine where the button would be positioned. The button represents who would actually be the dealer if Wendy was not there. The button happened to be two players to Todd's right which put him in the big blind for the one hundred dollars. The cards were dealt (two to each player) and before he looked at his he glanced around the table to determine if he could read any of the players. He learned that some players will reveal their emotions by the way they act when they look at their hole cards. O.B. made a jester of getting ready to fold before his turn so he knew he was weak, or was he? This was the only player he picked up on.

He got three callers of one hundred dollars by the time it got to Scott who was the small blind and without hesitation raised it to four hundred dollars. It was now time for Todd to look at his. He slowly raised the corner of the first card and saw the ace of spade and then picked up the corner of the second one. He couldn't believe it was another black ace. The thought went through his head, "Did I look at the same card twice?" He then picked up the corner of both cards and to his delight found the ace of spade and the ace of club. He asked himself, "Is this possible on the very first hand dealt that I have pocket aces? What are the odds of that, one hundred, two hundred to one or more?" He glanced over to Scott to see if he could pick up on something but he sat there like a mannequin with no emotion what so ever. He quickly analyzed the situation and came to the conclusion that he had the best hand going in and the best Scott could have is the pocket red aces, also there were three other callers before Scott's raise so they have to have something, maybe an ace queen or small pairs. If one of them has an ace then Scott would have to have a big pair, maybe kings.

Scott spoke up and asked if he was going to call or fold so Todd quickly raised his four hundred to eight hundred. He didn't know if that was the right thing to do but after Scott's remark he felt the pressure to keep the game moving.

The first and third caller folded promptly but the second player called the raise without blinking an eye. Now it was Scott's turn to fold, call or re-raise. He looked at his cards several times and with some hesitation called Todd's eight hundred dollars.

Todd felt strongly that Scott did not have the red aces. Wendy tapped the palm of her right hand on the table indicating that she would turn the three cards (referred to as the flop). The first card off the deck is discarded face down. This card is referred to by some as a discard, burned or buried card. The next three cards are turned and to Todd's amazement the flop showed the ace of heart, king of heart and king of spade giving him a full house. This confirmed his suspicion about Scott not having the two red aces but he could not dismiss the possibility of him having the other two kings. He had to wait until Scott made a play and then decide to either just call or raise. He knew he was in for the long haul no matter what he bet. A hand like this could very well cripple your bank roll but he knew very well he had to hang ten and ride the wave regardless.

Several times Scott looked at the flop then at his cards. The thought of him setting the ultimate trap flashed through Todd's mind making him breathe a little shallow. Thirty seconds went by but to Todd it seemed like an hour. His mouth began to dry out so he nervously picked up his drink and took a large swallow. As he placed his drink back in the bottle holder he noticed that Scott was watching him. Another long thirty seconds went by and then suddenly he saw one thousand dollars in chips being shoved into the center of the table. It was now up to Todd to make his move. He began to think the worse, figuring Scott had the other two kings. "I'm screwed!" He thought to himself, "I get this beautiful hand and I'm going to lose several thousand dollars on the very first hand of the game: what a bummer. I have to call; I can't fold a full house. My only hope is that he doesn't have quads." He decided to call Scott's bet and picked up what he thought was a thousand dollars and threw it reluctantly in front of him.

The third player quickly folded and it came around to Scott. He threw in an additional one thousand and said with a wry smile, "I see that you raised me, you must have a pretty powerful hand."

"I did? Aw man, I just wanted to call your bet," replied Todd.

Wendy immediately joined the conversation by telling Todd that the raise must stand since it was on the table and in front of his cards even though he did not announce it.

As fourth street card was about to be turned Todd realized he made a terrible mistake. He was almost sure Scott had the four kings and decided to fold his full house if Scott bets more that one hundred dollars. He now knew he was sucked in and suddenly realized he was at a table with players just as good as any on tour.

Wendy buried a card and flipped up the fourth card. Bingo! It was the fourth ace.

Todd could hardly contain himself for he had the nuts. Nothing could beat him now and the river card didn't matter. He had this hand no matter what. Now it was his turn to play the trap game. No matter what Scott did he would play it cool until the river card was dealt hoping that card would help his opponent if, in fact, he needed help.

It didn't take Scott long to check his hand and Todd did likewise.

"Hmm," murmured Scott, "Looks like that ace didn't help you."

Wendy quickly flipped up the river (fifth) card and it was a rag (better known as a no account small ranked card).

Scott sat there motionless for a solid two minutes but this no longer mattered to Todd for he wanted Scott to think he had the best hand. It was very difficult for him to not show any emotions. He concentrated on breathing normally and sat very still in his chair. Finally Scott picked up twenty five hundred dollars and very carefully stacked them in the middle of the table. He looked at Todd and said, "I strongly suggest you fold your hand son. I think you were chasing and I wouldn't want you to go home early."

"Contrary to your beliefs Scott," replied Todd. He paused for a few seconds and said "I really think I have you beat so I will raise your bet to five thousand." He then leaned back in his chair and smiled with the confidence of an African lion overlooking his harem of female lions.

Now it was Scott's turn to sweat. He rubbed his chin with his hand then stood up and walked behind his chair. "You're full with aces aren't you?" Pausing for a few seconds, he sat back down in his chair and placed his chin on the palms of his hands. "I got most of my money invested in the very first hand and I can't walk away from it now; I think I got you beat but then there's the possibility that you got a tweak better hand. What are the odds of you having four aces while I'm sitting here with four kings: wouldn't that be a phenomenal circumstance? That would be one for Doyle Brunson's book."

Todd was getting a little impatient with Scott's delay of the game. As a matter of fact the other players were also, but being a new member at the table he felt somewhat reluctant to say anything. Finally O.B. spoke up, "Scottie, you're going to call the young man so I don't see why you just don't throw in your chips so we can keep the game going."

Scott apologized to O.B. and abruptly called the raise. Before the chips settled on the table Todd's aces were flipped up. In unison the whole table including Wendy cried out, "Son-of-a-bitch, he had them!"

Flipping over his kings Scott said in a voice depicting disappointment, "You want to see something bizarre? Look at this."

Again, in unison everyone said, "Son-of-a-bitch he had quads!" The whole table was stunned.

Tom looked across the table at a dejected Scott and said, "I've been playing poker for more years than I can remember and over all those years I never saw anything like what just happened here. Talk about bad beats, this is the worst one I've ever seen and probably will ever see. The only thing that tops this is the power both of you had on the very first hand of the game. This is one for the books."

O.B. chuckled and said, "I'd ask everyone to take a small break to freshen their drinks but I notice no one started on their first one, in fact, the ice hasn't even started to melt."

As Todd was stacking his chips Wendy began shuffling the cards for the next hand.

For the rest of the evening Todd played it tight and close to the vest and when the game ended he went home eight thousand dollars richer. It could have probably been more but he became much too conservative.

Chapter Four

Everything seemed to go Todd's way over the next few months. He was sitting on the thirty-three thousand including the eight thousand he won in Baltimore and was doing quite well in the local hold-em tournaments. The payouts weren't large, anywhere from four hundred to twelve hundred dollars, but they all added up and it kept him competitively sharp for the big ones that he hoped to get in.

He landed a job with a local printing company as an account executive. He was under the tutelage of the senior account executive who retired six months later. Todd was liked so well by everyone he was given the retiree's accounts to work. This immediately increased his earnings to six figures, far beyond what he ever expected.

The following year he and Debbie were married and they spent their honeymoon in Lauderdale by the sea in Florida.

At first they rented an apartment but one year later Debbie became pregnant with their son so they decided on buying a house immediately to begin raising their family. Over the next five years they were blessed with two more children, another boy and a girl.

With the money Todd was making as an account executive it was not necessary for Debbie to begin her career until all the children were in school. She was in no hurry for she wanted to be a mother first.

During this time the game of Texas Hold-em dropped on Todd's priority list but soon it would work its way back up because now at the age of thirty-one he began to realize the importance of being in his office every day instead of on the road servicing his accounts. With the new incentive plan the company presented him he accepted the position of regional manager without taking a cut in pay. Now that he had the luxury of a personal secretary and a junior executive to assist him there was a lot of free time for himself.

It was a Thursday afternoon, around three when his phone rang. He was surprise to hear O.B."s voice at the other end. "It took some doing but I tracked you down big guy," commented O.B., "We're still talking about that hand you had against Scottie: How long has it been, five or six years ago?"

Todd suddenly realized that five years flew by like the wind in a willow tree. The more he and O.B. talked the more the competitive juices began to flow throughout his body.

O.B. told him the reason for the call was to invite him to a no-limit game they were having on Sunday afternoon. Without first checking with his wife Todd immediately accepted his invitation.

That evening at the dinner table Debbie reminded him about the friends they were having over on Sunday for a cookout. "Oh hell!" he thought, "I forgot all about that." Before he realized what he was saying he told his wife that his number one salesman was home with the flu and it was necessary to drive to his office in Ithaca to write up a three year contract for him, a deal he actually closed the day before he got ill. He went on to say that the plant had to have it by Monday in order to meet the customer's deadline. This was the very first time he could recall that he lied to Debbie. He promised himself he would never do it again. It was the only way he knew how to get out of the Sunday cookout without hurting anyone's feelings.

He expected to get an argument from Debbie but being the good wife that she was, agreed that it was the right thing to do since it was part of his job. She said she would call their friends and postpone it until the next weekend.

He felt relieved that he didn't have to explain anything more to her but at the same time he was kicking himself in the ass for not 'fessing up' and telling her the truth. Little did he realize that this was the start of something that will eventually be like a run away freight train.

At twelve noon on Sunday and with ten thousand dollars in his pocket he was driving south to Baltimore instead of north to Ithaca as his wife was led to believe. The more he thought about the lie he told Debbie the more he passed it off as a poker bluff and soon accepted it as such.

This time it was not necessary to meet anyone. It was going to be at the same place he played some five plus years ago, at O.B.'s office.

When he arrived he noticed that the same players were there with the exception of one new player named Justin, a young man at about the same age he was when he first played at O.B.'s office.

O.B. took everyone's cash and in turn presented them with $10,000 in chips. With drinks in hand the players sat down at their assigned seats. The game was about to start. Once again Scott was sitting to the right of Todd and while they were waiting for Wendy to make her appearance the two of them talked about their first hand of the game some five years ago. Five minutes went by before one of the players asked if she was going to show up. At that very moment she walked in and apologized for being late.

She got tied up in traffic on the bay bridge. Todd noticed she did not look as nice as she did the first time he played and was told later that she had some medical problems.

The first hour of the game was a complete disaster for Todd. He refused to play junk cards and wouldn't you know that was the only cards that were flopped. Had he played the junk cards he would probably be up several thousand dollars but he kept telling himself it was the right thing to do in a game of this magnitude. Another half hour went by and the junk cards kept coming and coming until he felt compelled to at least see the flop.

The next hand dealt him was a seven and eight of club and he decided to venture a call to see what the flop would bring. He limped in for the big blind of one hundred dollars and was immediately greeted with a four hundred dollar raise by young Justin. There were two callers to Justin's raise before it got back to him. It was evident that he most definitely was holding the worst hand.

Todd counted his chips and at this juncture of the game he was down eight hundred dollars just in the forced bets. He had to cough up these blinds without even having an outside chance of winning a pot. He quickly calculated the amount of chips in the center of the table. The two players that called Justin's raise were the two blinds totaling one hundred and fifty dollars plus Todd's call of one hundred dollars plus Justin's raise to five hundred and the two callers for another eight hundred and fifty. There was sixteen hundred dollars already in the center of the table meaning there would be a four to one return if he called but did he want to risk it on suited connecters?

The longer he thought about it the more convinced he became to call the raise. He fumbled with his chips, stacking and re-stacking them until Justin finally called the clock on him.

Without thinking anymore about it Todd reluctantly threw in four one hundred dollar chips.

Wendy tapped the table with her hand, pushed aside the burn card face down and flopped the next three cards. They came up ace of club, ten of club and jack of club.

Todd winced inside, he knew he had a flush but did any of the other guys have one with him and if they did would they be holding the king, queen or nine?

The two blinds checked and now it was Todd's turn to either check or make a move. He took his time to think this out. He was concerned that one of the blinds could be holding the king of club hoping to suck out one more club for the nut flush or that he could already have the king with another club hoping to trap someone on the river card. On the other side of the coin he might have an ace hoping no one has a flush drawl. There were so many variables it made his head spin. And what about Justin to his left, the one that raised pre-flop? What was he so proud of? He could only speculate that he had a pocket pair. Even now if he had a set a seasoned player would probably back off the flopped clubs if someone makes a hefty bet.

Justin spoke up, "I'm sorry Todd but you're really holding up the game. I'm calling the clock on you again."

Without any hesitation Todd threw in five-hundred dollars. It was an investment he had to make to find out where everyone stood with their hand.

Justin looked at Todd, smiled and said, "Is that a 'feeler' bet? I think you're chasing a club. If I hit on the river your flush will be down the drain as it were, no pun intended, I'll call your five-hundred."

To Todd's delight the two blinds folded. He now knew that his flush was good at this point but he had fourth street and the river card to sweat out. It was evident that Justin was sitting on a set of aces, jacks or tens but witch one?

With both blinds folded it was up to Todd to check or bet. He chose to gamble and tossed four hundred dollars in the center of the table and was quickly called by Justin. He was relieved that it was not raised and now knew his flush was the best hand. The only concern he now had was what would be turned on the next two cards.

Fourth street showed the deuce of heart which was no threat so he bet eight hundred dollars. Now it was Justin stacking and shuffling his chips. Todd gave it a few minutes and called the clock on Justin. "Sorry Justin," said Todd with a smile, "We should keep the game moving." It felt so good for him to reverse the pressure.

Calling the clock on Justin may have been the wrong thing to do for he was greeted with an eight hundred dollar raise.

Todd quickly got to his feet and looked up to the ceiling. "What the hell kind of bet is that? I know you don't have a flush! Your best hand is a set and I'm willing to bet on that. You have to put me on a flush. I'm sure I got you, I call"!

Justin sat motionless in his chair and offered no comment.

Wendy tapped the table, set the burn card aside and turned the four of club.

The last thing Todd wanted to see was another club so he quickly checked his hand and looked to Justin for any sign of emotion.

Justin looked straight ahead then down at his cards, checking and rechecking them. Finally he looked over to Todd's stack of chips and then back at his. In a calm voice he asked Todd to give him a chip count.

Todd began to laugh and said, "You're not serious I hope, hell, you're not putting me all in and you know it so what's the point? Don't try to buy this pot."

Justin quickly counted Todd's chips and looked over to Wendy, "I'm putting Todd all in."

Wendy looked at Todd and said, "You've been put all in. Do you opt to call or fold"?

It had been nothing but a nightmare for Todd every since he sat down at the table. He couldn't remember the last time he felt helpless in a card game. Beads of sweat began to form on his brow. He hoped no one would notice but it was quite obvious to everyone. He had to make a major decision. If he was wrong it would be a long ride home and he wasn't ready for that but if he was right he would have a nice healthy stack of chips to play with for the balance of the game. He kept telling himself to fold the flush but he was so sure Justin was sitting on a set. He took one last look at his opponent but saw nothing but a stone face. Before he realized it he turned over his cards and blurted out the words, "I call"!

Before turning over his cards Justin looked over at Todd and calmly commented, "You were wrong about me having a set, I only have a pair of kings and I would have bet you were flushed. You had me up to fourth street but the river killed you." He turned over his kings.

The blood drained from Todd's head as he stared at the king of spade and king of club.

"That's it gentleman, said Todd, "I'm busted." He got up from his chair, put on his jacket and started for the door.

O.B. called out to him as he opened the door. "Before you leave could I have a few words with you"?

No one at the table could hear the conversation between the two but when they saw O.B. reach in his pocket and take out a wad of bills it was quite evident he offered Todd a loan.

They knew for sure when Todd returned to the table and handed Wendy five thousand dollars for more chips.

The rest of the game was as much of a disaster for Todd as the beginning. He kept telling himself that the game would turn around in his favor eventually each time he asked O.B. for another loan. When the game broke up he realized he not only lost the $10,000 he brought with him he now owed $15,000 in loans. What was more sickening was his promise to repay the man in one week.

While driving home he began to think of things he could tell Debbie. She was surely going to ask why he was home so soon. He decided to tell her that when he arrived in Ithaca he found his salesman in the office. He felt much better and was just finishing up the contract as he walked in. He would also tell her that he was invited home for dinner and then headed back home. "That should be convincing enough," he thought. His mind kept racing, "She doesn't know about the ten thousand I took with me and I have until next week to get the money to O.B.." He was content at this moment not to think about that part, after all, that was seven days away.

Chapter Five

Things went off without a hitch. Debbie believed his story and everything was lovey-dovey at the home front.

Monday morning arrived and Todd was at his desk preparing for a meeting with management when his secretary told him there was a call from someone named Scott. He thought it was one of his salesman's clients and, with a cheery voice said, "Hello Scott, how may I help you"? "I don't think you realize who you're talking to Todd, this is the poker Scott calling." "Don't tell me you guys got another game planned so soon," Todd replied with a chuckle, "If you do I don't think I'll be able to make it. I got fifteen big ones to pay back to O.B."

There was a pause at the other end of the line, then in a solemn voice Scott said, "That's who I'm calling about. O.B. bought the farm on the 695 bypass early this morning. A semi ass-ended him and rammed him into a stalled car. He didn't have a chance."

It took a while for all of this to sink into Todd's brain. There was unbroken silence between the two until Scott finally asked him if he was still there. "Yes, I'm here. I can't believe what you just told me, my God what a tragedy!"

"There's something else I got to tell you Todd. O.B. didn't

have the money everyone thought he had. He actually cashed in his life insurance policy a while back to make ends meet. You happened to catch him at the right time when he loaned you the fifteen thousand. O.B.'s wife is going to need that money to give him a decent burial. Little did she know he squandered their life's saving on these big poker games he's been hosting plus his trips to Atlantic City. Somehow you've got to get that money back to her in the next day or two. What do you want me to tell her"?

There was a pause at Todd's end of the line. He was trying to think of how he could raise the money that quickly. He had to tell Scott something. Finally he said without knowing why he said it, "Tell O.B,'s wife I'll have it in the mail tomorrow first thing."

"Great"! Scott replied, "She'll be very happy and relieved to hear this. I'll be talking to you later to let you know when and where the funeral will be held if you're interested in coming, goodbye."

It was now time for Todd to start worrying about how he was going to raise fifteen thousand dollars by tomorrow. Small beads of perspiration formed on his forehead and under his nose. He thought about asking his dad but he knew that his parents just bought a condominium in South Carolina so he was surely tapped out. It was useless to try for a loan at the bank since he already had a second mortgage on the house for the swimming pool and both of his credit cards were maxed out. He thought about asking the owner of the company he worked for but dismissed that thought immediately because he knew he was ultra conservative and would be looked upon him as a poor manager of money. This could jeopardize his job and he certainly didn't want that to happen. He was most definitely between a rock and a hard place.

It was a very stressful evening at home. He rarely spoke to Debbie or the children. Finally at bedtime his wife asked what was bothering him and he replied that it was a difficult day at work and let it go at that. Without pursuing it any further Debbie rolled on her side and said goodnight.

The next day was like most other days at the office, business as usual, except for the constant worry of how he was going to get a check for fifteen thousand dollars in the mail to O.B.'s wife. It was ten in the morning when he got a call from one of his biggest customers. It was an emergency call and his customer was panicking. It seems that the person at the other end of the line left his inventory run dangerously low and was calling for help. He pleaded to Todd to help him out with a seven working day delivery. If he didn't get it in house by then he would lose his job. Todd told him to keep calm and he would get back to him within the hour.

He immediately phoned Joe the plant manager at their Scranton plant. Joe owed Todd a big favor for bailing him out of a problem several months ago. He told Todd he would definitely come through for him even if he had to move some things around to get it out of the door. Problem solved.

Suddenly a light went on in his brain. He immediately called his customer and told him that the complete job would come to $32,000 plus a rush service charge of $3,200 but if he could prepay the $32,000 he could waive the rush service charge. His customer was so elated with the news he told him to stop by over lunch and pick up the check.

On the way back he stopped at the bank his company did business with and presented the check for cash. He did this several times before for his boss so he knew they would not question the transaction. All he had to do was sign his name and the $32,000 was his. He had at least 52 days to return the money before it would have to be accounted for, seven days of production time plus another forty-five days before the money had to be presented for payment. He had plenty of time now, or did he?

He then went to his personal bank and purchased a cashier's check for $15,000 and returned to the office. After several tries he finally got Scott on the phone and told him he had the money for O.B.'s wife. He got her address and immediately mailed it that same afternoon. As he was driving he suddenly realized he had $17,000 cash in his coat pocket. He decided to place this money in an old envelope he found in the glove compartment and hide it in the trunk of the car for safe keeping. He would decide later what to do with it but right now he wanted to enjoy a relaxing evening with his family. The evening meal prepared for him was excellent and after dinner he and Debbie sat by the fireplace and sipped wine. With the pressure off him for the moment, Todd enjoyed a perfect evening.

The following day his boss stopped by the office to congratulate him for the nice $32,000 order he got and also to tell him that he was needed at the Philadelphia office to help the new recently hired salesman get set up with his assigned accounts. He was told that it would probably take at least a week to get him started. If he left tomorrow which was Wednesday he could count on being back home by next Thursday.

That evening his wife packed his cloths for the trip and the next morning he was headed eastward to the city of brotherly love.

When he arrived he was surprised to see the new office in an orderly fashion. The new salesman had worked for a competitor for over ten years and knew what had to be done. He even interviewed several secretaries and had one picked out to start work first thing Monday morning. The only thing remaining to be done was go over the accounts which took only a few hours. The new man was well versed and knowledgeable of the company's products. This turned out to be a walk in the park for Todd. By Friday afternoon there was nothing left to do. The new salesman had to leave early for Dayton to help his wife prepare for their move to Philadelphia. This left Todd with nothing to do until next Wednesday. Suddenly he realized that Atlantic City was nearby and he had the $17,000 in the trunk of his car. He got that urge to play hold-em and convinced himself that he could go to Atlantic City and win back the $15,000 he borrowed from the company. He figured as soon as he got back to the office next Thursday he could replace the money and no one would be any the wiser. He felt strongly that this was the answer to his dilemma. How much worse could it be if he was caught defrauding the company for $15,000 or $32,000?

By 7 p.m. he finished his evening meal along with a few cocktails at the casino lounge. With $17,000 in chips he walked to the tables looking for a Texas hold-em no limit game with $100 and $200 blinds. It didn't take very long to find a table with an empty seat.

After an hour of playing he found himself winning around $1,500. At this rate it would take ten hours to get the money he needed so he decided to play a little looser in hopes he would get lucky. Hands that would normally be mucked he played in hopes of catching the other players off guard. On one hand he got pocket threes and played the hand out to the river in hopes of getting a set but it didn't happen and he soon lost the $1,500 he was up. Sometimes this works but most of the time it doesn't. He was even one hand and out the other. It was like this for the next several hours and he became so frustrated he attempted bluffs and was caught each time. The other players at the table quickly picked up on what he was doing and took every advantage of it.

At 2;30 the next morning a haggard and pitiful man stood up from the table with just a $100 chip in his hand. He cleared his throat and with a cracked voice said, "Gentleman when it gets around to me I will be all in with my last chip." He was dealt a five and seven off suit but never got any help from the flop that were all face cards. Fourth street and the river cards were of no help either. Without saying a word he walked away and left the casino. Driving back to his hotel in Philadelphia gave him time to contemplate just how much trouble he had caused not only himself but his family. He got so ill from thinking about it he had to pull off the road and threw up. He well knew his back was against the wall and there was no solution to a problem that began when he accepted the $15,000 loan from O.B. He should have realized right there and then not to accept a loan that could not be paid back as promised. Had he walked away from that game with a $10,000 loss he wouldn't be in this trouble.

He stayed in his motel all day Saturday with that miserable and sickening feeling eating at his guts. When he awoke Sunday morning he felt worse than the day before. Guilt, remorse and the hating of one's self for being so stupid only compounded the feelings he had the day before. Unable to eat breakfast and barely finishing one cup of coffee he went to the lobby phone and left a voice mail message at the Philadelphia office stating that he was headed back home. With all that has happened to him he completely forgot he had already phoned the same message from Atlantic City.

The trip back home was long and arduous. It was very difficult for him to keep his mind on driving and it caused him to have two near accidents. His nerves were more than he could handle while driving so he pulled to the side of the highway in an effort to collect himself. It took about thirty minutes before he was able to commence driving,

While on the road he began talking to himself, "$32,000 is not a tremendous amount of money but who would loan it to me without some sort of collateral? That's the key, collateral! Who would loan me that amount of money without some sort of insurance of ever getting it back? Wait a minute; I remember O.B. telling me about the guy that played at his games called Chris. He always borrowed money from some guy in Baltimore to get in his games. He got in trouble several times for not paying the money back on time but managed somehow to get it paid. This might be the answer, at least for the time being. I'll worry about that when the time comes, first things first."

Once again he pulled to the side of the road to check his cell phone for Scott's number. He would ask him if he might know Chris' phone number. Scott's line was busy but after several tries he finally reached him. Luckily Scott had Chris' number and Todd dialed him immediately.

Chris was happy to hear from him and said he would introduce him to the guy anytime. "What about today"? Todd asked. "Let me make a call and I'll get right back to you," replied Chris.

Less than ten minutes later the cell phone rang. "Hey Todd how soon can you get here"?

Todd told him to give him at least two hours and to meet him at the same restaurant at the Inner Harbor where he first met the guys.

One hour and forty minutes later he pulled into a parking space by the Inner Harbor restaurant. Before he had time to turn off the engine Chris popped into the front seat.

After a few words of greeting Todd put the car in gear and waited for Chris to give him directions then drove out of the parking lot.

Following the directions he realized they were crossing the Francis Scott Key Bridge and after several left and right turns he was told to pull up in front of a magnificent townhouse.

Several minutes after the door bell rang an over weight black woman opened the door and greeted them with a broad smile.

She looked exactly like the black mammy in the old movie Gone With The Wind.

"Well look who's here! If it isn't Mr. Chris! How are you?"

Chris replied with a smile, "I'm just fine Miss Jessica and you look bright eyed and bushy tailed."

With a big belly laugh she said, "Oh Mr. Chris, how you go on. Come on in and bring your friend."

The two followed Jessica through the hall. She opened the door to a large room that immediately presented itself as the office of the person that would hopefully loan Todd the money he so desperately needed.

Sitting behind a huge oak desk was an older black man, probably in his late sixties. He was elegantly dressed and wore a bright red satin smoking jacket. Without a word being said he merely pointed to two chairs indicating that they should sit down.

As they were taking their seats Todd noticed two men entering the room. They all appeared to have pumped iron most of their lives. They wore short sleeved shirts, apparently to show off their biceps and to strike fear into the hearts of a potential borrower and it obviously worked because Todd found himself swallowing the lump in his throat.

Finally the guy behind the desk spoke. "Well Chris it's good to see you again. As you already know I don't take social calls this time of the day so I'm assuming either you or your friend is in need of some money. What is your friend's name"?

Chris smiled and replied, "Mr. Skinnerbache, how are you today? My friend is in need of some money and his name is Todd. It's an emergency loan to bail him out of a monster problem. Todd this is Mr. Jake Skinnerbache."

Skinnerbache glanced over in Todd's direction and said, "Spare me the details of the monster problem you're in young man, just fill out this paper giving me your full name, address and phone number, your place of employment, work phone number and annual salary. If you don't want to give up all this just say so and leave. Do you understand all that"?

Todd thought for a few moments then reached over, picked up the blank paper and told Skinnerbache he had no problem in giving out that information. Although he hated to implicate his family and reveal the information of his employer he had no other recourse except to walk away and face the music with the authorities back home. He wasn't ready for that.

Asked how much money he needed Todd replied in a sheepish tone that the amount was $32,000.

Skinnerbache quickly replied that he did not loan money in increments of $2,000 nor did he like to loan out $40,000. If he needed $32,000 he would have to take $50,000.

It didn't take a math genius to figure out that Skinnerbache wanted a big return on his investment and $50,000 seemed like the right figure.

Todd knew what was going down but figured he would just squirrel the $18,000 and return it with the balance he owed. He accepted the $50,000 without asking what the interest rate would be which was another horrible blunder on his part.

Before he realized it one of the muscle men was counting out the money and placed it in his hand.

As soon as the last bill was placed in Todd's hand Skinnerbache told him he now owed him $65,000 and was payable in full exactly thirty days from today.

Todd winced, "Wait a minute Mr. Skinnerbache that's thirty per cent per month. I don't think I can afford this loan. Take it back and let me think about it for a day or two."

One of the muscled goons stepped up and got into Todd's face. "Look Mac, you accepted the loan. If you want to pay it back right now its still 65G's. Is that what you want to do"?

Todd looked over at Chris as though to say, "What the hell did you get me into"?

Chris shrugged his shoulders and said, "I thought you knew about these things man."

There was not a word spoken between the two on their way back to Todd's car.

As Todd was getting out of the car Chris finally said, "Hey buddy I don't think this turned out to be a good idea for you. I would have said something but I truthfully thought you knew the loan shark's interest rate in the city. Try to get the money back to them in thirty days or they'll come after you. They'll use all the information you gave them to the fullest extent so don't get cute with them. Good luck."

The drive home seemed shorter than anticipated. Once home he would have to face his wife who had the uncanny ability to know immediately when something was wrong.

Ten miles outside of town he made the decision to pull into the nearest motel and stay the night. The next morning he could arrive home just in time to ready himself for work. If he timed it right he could be in and out before she could suspect anything.

Chapter Six

Things went well at home the next morning and he was on his way to the office. Upon arriving he immediately took the $32,000 to the accounting department before his boss could suspect anything. Somewhat relieved he walked to his office and sat behind his desk to finish his coffee.

His secretary walked in and handed him several phone messages. As she was leaving she told him that his boss would not be in until late morning and wanted to see him as soon as he got in.

Todd asked her if she knew what he wanted to see him about but she didn't know. Thinking that it was surely about company business he cleared his desk and proceeded to return the calls that his secretary gave him. It was good to get back into the swing of things again for it gave him a break from thinking of the $65,000.

It was now 11:30 and he finished returning his last phone call. He decided if Tony, his boss, was not back by noon he would drive across town to his favorite Greek restaurant for one of their delicious salads.

At 12 o'clock he put his jacket on and started to leave for

lunch. As he walked down the hall he heard his name called. It was Tony, "Todd, don't leave just yet we have to talk."

"Be right with you," replied Todd, "Give me a minute to grab a coke."

In a very serious voice Tony said, "Now Todd, forget the coke!"

As soon as he entered Tony's office he was told to close the door behind him. He knew something was seriously wrong but never imagined it could be about the $32,000.

Tony immediately picked up the phone and dialed a number.

Todd could hardly make out what he was saying. He managed to catch the last few words, "Is it there?" and "When did you get it?"

Tony sat back in his chair and looked straight at Todd. It seemed an eternity before he said anything. Finally he spoke, "Have you anything you should tell me Todd?"

"No, nothing of any importance," answered Todd, "Other than I just got back from Philly but of course you knew that already. What's up boss?"

Tony got up from his chair and gazed out the window with his back to Todd and in a somber voice said, "Just as I was leaving home this morning I got a call from our new salesman. He was wondering why you suddenly decided not to show up at the office this morning. After listening to the phone messages from you he was concerned that he may have said or done something that didn't meet with your approval. Also last Friday I took a phone call from one of our customers, ECI, Inc. He wanted to thank you for the favor you did for him. Seems as though you got him an emergence delivery and saved him somewhere in the neighborhood of $3,000 by paying cash up front. This got me to thinking since our company policy is to never charge any of our customers for emergency delivery service and most of all never to ask for up front money. On the way to the office this morning I stopped by our bank and found out you cashed a company check in the amount of $32,000. That was the ECI, Inc. check and no one authorized you to cash any checks of any kind in the past month or so. I just checked with our accounting department and they told me just this morning you presented them with $32,000 cash and instructed them to credit ECI, Inc. for that amount. Last but no less important I know you went to Atlantic City with that money. How do I know? You called the Philly office from there and it showed up on the caller ID. All this being said I come to the conclusion you gambled with company money at least once, maybe more and I have a gut feeling you have a problem. Am I right or wrong? You don't have to answer that question because at this point in time it doesn't matter. Todd, it is my duty to tell you that you are terminated as of this moment. We do not tolerate any employee that is untrustworthy. We always thought of you as a valuable member of this organization and had big plans for you but you let us down. Mr. Breame will accompany you to your desk where you will pick up your personal things and vacate the building."

Tony never turned from the window to face the man he accused but this was okay with Todd because he knew his boss had him dead to rights and it would have been very difficult to look into the eyes of the man that helped him get to where he used to be with this company.

There was a knock on the door. Tony turned around and walked to the door with his head down. There stood Mr. Breame ready to escort Todd to his desk.

Chapter Seven

Most of the day he drove around the area but not straying too far from home. At times he would stop at an out of the way bar for a drink hoping he could come up with something to tell the family.

It was now late in the afternoon and he headed for home. His decision was not to say anything about his dismissal in hopes he could land a job before the family became suspicious.

Prior to entering his front door Todd made every effort to appear as though it was just another ordinary day at the office. As always he placed his attaché case by the coat tree and called out, "Hey family I'm home. What's for dinner?"

He waited for a reply but there was nothing but silence. Once again he called out, "Anybody home? What's for dinner?"

Finally the silence was broken. It was Debbie's voice from the study down the hallway. "Todd, come to the study. We need to talk."

Due to one too many gin and tonics he never realized that anything was wrong. As he entered the study Todd saw his wife sitting on the foot stool by the fire place. He leaned over to give her a kiss and asked where the kids were.

Debbie leaned back to avoid the on coming kiss and told him they were with their grandparents.

She now began crying as she told him Tony had called earlier while she was out and left a message on the answering machine, "I want you to hear the message," she blurted out, "Then tell me what the hell happened."

The blood drained from his head and the sense of sobriety became prominent as he walked slowly to the phone. He knew the word was out about his termination. He had only hoped it could have come from him at the proper time and place. This was no way for her to find something like this out without some sort of an explanation.

Todd hesitated for several seconds until he developed enough courage to press the voice mail button. "Todd, this is Tony. Your final paycheck will be mailed to you at the end of the week. It will include your salary, commissions and all the monies from your retirement fund. We request you do not return this call or stop by at any time."

There was nothing the man could do but come clean and tell his wife everything. The worst part of the confession was the debt to the loan shark but he knew this had to be told also. He could see how distraught Deb was and could only hope for her forgiveness.

She slowly arose from the foot stool then quickly left the room without saying a word or even looking at him.

He could hear her sobbing as she climbed the stairs to the bedroom and decided it best not to follow her. Instead he went to the downstairs guest room where he stayed for the rest of the night.

Early the next morning he awoke with the aroma of bacon frying in the kitchen. With no dinner the night before he was famished and hunger drove him to once again face his wife in hopes somehow she would forgive him for his stupidity.

He anticipated her coming down on him hard but to his surprise she asked him to sit at the table while she prepared his breakfast before she left to pick up the children at their grandparents and take them to school.

When he finished eating Deb poured a cup of coffee and sat on the other side of the table facing him straight on and finally spoke. "I don't know if you deserve another chance or not Todd but I'm giving you one never the less. I don't know how but you've got to get us out of this mess. You found a way into it now find a way out. I don't know how you're going to do it without a job but that's your problem. If you do somehow accomplish it and you promise never to play poker again then, and only then, will our marriage continue is that clear?"

With a sigh of relief Todd promised her he would find a job and have this cleared up in no time.

Chapter Eight

The first thing Todd did that day was to stop at his bank and apply for an equity loan on his home but soon found out a couple hours later that he was not eligible since his equity did not meet the $65,000 he applied for and surprisingly they already knew about his loss of employment. He wondered how the bank knew about his termination so soon and then realized he got his company credit card through this bank and Tony apparently had it canceled as of yesterday.

He had no one to go to for this kind of money not even his parents. Even if his parents could have helped him it would be his very last resort.

He bought a newspaper and stopped by a small restaurant for coffee. While there he scanned the employment section but found nothing,

The next thing was to stop by the employment agency office. All he got there were leads that paid very little or were out of the realms of his expertise.

He began to realize that getting back on track was not as easy as he thought it might be. Suddenly he realized that in the trunk of his car was $18,000 of the loan he got in Baltimore. Because of what happened the day before at the office and having to face his wife he completely forgot about it.

The urge to play 'Hold-em' started to take over and all that he promised his wife quickly vanished from his mind. He was sure this would be the answer to all his problems. This time he was so sure he could quadruple his money at Atlantic City then drive to Baltimore and pay off the $65,000. His devious mind began to plan just how he would do this without Deb becoming suspicious.

Deb picked up the children and arrived home a few minutes after Todd. After the kids got settled in and were up in their bedrooms doing their homework Todd spoke up. "Honey, I got some good news. I got an interview with a company in Horsham, PA. I spoke with them on the phone earlier and they want to set up an office in this area. I would be doing the very same thing I did before. With salary and commission I would be making almost the same income as before. This is a luncheon interview so I have to leave in time to be there by twelve thirty tomorrow."

She once again believed her husband not knowing he told her a bald-faced lie without showing any signs of guilt. Earlier in their marriage he would have never thought of lying to her but now it started to come easier and easier each time.

There was no doubt in Todd's mind that he could return from Atlantic City free and clear of all the monies owed. He then could concentrate on obtaining another job or maybe even starting his own business. He slept well that night quite content that the following day would be the start of his journey back to a normal life with his family.

By 10 a.m. he was on his way to Atlantic City. The closer he got to the casino the more the juices in his body began to flow. Just the thought of sitting at the table and raking in a huge pile of chips made him more anxious to get there. Due to heavy traffic he did not arrive until 1:30 p.m.

Without hesitation he bought some chips and placed the balance of his money in the inside pocket of his jacket. Thinking it wise to start at a smaller game he sat at a $5 and $10 blind table. If the cards were good to him he would move to a $100/$200 game. This way he could determine if the poker Gods were with him and not lose a lot of money.

In less than forty-five minutes he was up over $1,500. The cards were falling just right for him. He was either hitting inside straights or catching the flush card on the river.

He kept telling himself this was finally the day he would be free of debt. The nightmares in his life over the past weeks would no longer exist.

He decided to play at this table for another thirty minutes. If he could win at least another thousand dollars it would be time to move on to bigger stakes. Exactly twenty five minutes later Todd walked away from the table up $2,800.

He found the table he was looking for, one with $100/200 blinds, and immediately claimed the only open seat available. Knowing he needed more than the money he had in chips he immediately bought additional chips with all the money he had with him.

As he sat down he noticed there were two women at the table. He quickly realized by their healthy chip stacks they were not 'dead money'. This was a first time for Todd to play against the fairer sex so he decided to check them out for a couple hands. He kept mucking his cards until he was obligated to lay down a blind giving him the opportunity to observe the other players.

When it was his turn to post the small blind he looked at his two down cards and found a miserable three and five unsuited. Normally one would muck these cards but Todd remembered the belly busting straights he hit at the last table and since no one raised the bet, which indicated weakness, he decided to call the big blind just to find out if his luck would carry over from the last table.

The big blind checked and the flop came up ace, four, deuce unsuited. It took some doing but Todd showed no emotion to the baby straight he was now in possession of. He checked in hopes someone would bet. If they did he would come back over the top with a healthy raise.

Sure enough the big blind bet four hundred dollars and everyone behind him mucked their cards. It was now up to Todd to make his move. He figured the big blind for a pair of aces and at the most, a set.

Todd did his best to look concerned with the four hundred dollar bet. He sat there several minutes without moving a muscle. Finally the big blind spoke up and said with a smile, "Hey buddy there's three things you can do, one is to call the other is fold or you could raise me. I really hope you do the latter."

Todd did not look up or acknowledge his comment in any way. He just sat there trying to figure out how much he could get this guy for without scaring him off. Finally he announced that he was raising the bet. He counted out the original four hundred dollar bet and followed up with an additional thousand dollars and was immediately called.

Fourth street was turned up showing a king of spade. Todd bet one thousand dollars and again was called immediately. The river showed a jack of club and the bet again was one thousand dollars which was immediately called by the big blind.

Showing pride in what he thought was a 'slow play and trap' the guy smiled and turned over a pair of aces only to be stunned at the three and five Todd turned over.

The guy to Todd's right chuckled and said, "Partner you played your hand as well as it could possibly be played, good hand my man."

The poker gods and lady luck could not have been kinder to Todd. For the next several hours he could do nothing wrong. Some of the players left the table either tapped out or in fear of him.

His chip stacks, each in their individual denomination, were stacked neatly in front of him. He didn't know how much he was up and refused to count his chips to find out for this is a superstition of many poker players. If you count them it could be followed by a period of bad luck. He knew one thing for sure; it wasn't enough to cover his debt.

After several bottles of water Todd realized he could no longer avoid visiting the men's room. Leaving the table could very possibly disrupt the grace of the poker gods but Mother Nature also had a say in the matter.

Before returning to the table he decided to walk outside for some fresh air. Being away from the noise of the casino was a good time to phone his wife and tell her he was running late with the job interview, an excuse she would surely accept. He told her if it got too late he would stay over and return home the following day. This was a good out in case he needed the extra time.

With a combination of luck, skill and strategy Todd continued to win. He now realized that he was destined to be a big winner no matter what was dealt to him so he decided to let it all hang out and go for the gusto. It was his day, if he folded it was a good lay down, if he called he was fortunate enough to catch the right card and ultimately win a healthy pot.

Several hours later he became curious about the amount of chips stacked in front of him. Without counting them he knew he was well over the $65,000 needed to pay off that scum bag Skinnerbache.

Some of the players at the table decided to leave. Several lost all their money while others figured Todd was too hot to beat.

Their seats were promptly taken by several young men. They didn't appear to be old enough to have earned enough money in their lifetime to afford sitting at this table but here they were with thousands of dollars worth of chips. They addressed each other as 'young guns'.

The strategy of the game completely changed. The 'young guns' were not content to just limp in with rags; they would automatically raise the big blind which made them dangerous, very dangerous.

Todd knew he had to change his game and be patient until he had a power hand to call with. This was the only way to beat these young punks and take them for all their chips.

For a solid hour he would fold hand after hand, even giving up his blind chips. Finally a hand came; it was a pair of kings. The blind was raised to $400 by one of the 'young guns' followed with an additional $400 by one of other 'young guns'. Todd quickly counted their remaining chips and went all in. Everyone folded but the two raisers. It took approximately fifteen seconds for the first one to throw in his remaining $5,600 and less time for the other to call with his last $7,200. Todd pulled back all except $7,200 of his chips and dealer then divided the chips in two piles, one amounting to $16,800 and another amounting to $3,200.

The dealer then instructed the three players to turn over their cards. The first 'young gun' showed a pair of threes and the second one a pair of jacks, the only legitimate calling hand of the two. It didn't seem to bother them in the least when Todd laid down his pair of kings. The one young player chuckled and commented, "Hey man, you know what they say, any hand is just as good as all the others before the flop." Todd smiled and replied, "You're right, but I feel much more comfortable with my kings."

The flop was revealed and Todd's heart sank. In the middle of the table lay an ace, a three and a jack; both 'young guns' hit for a set. Fourth street did not help anyone with a 4 of spade. The guy holding the set of jacks started counting the chips in anticipation of raking in a nice $20,000 pot but was shocked when a king popped up on the river. Without any comment the two walked away from the table. The sporting thing to do was shake Todd's hand which you probably would have seen with the older and more seasoned players. Their seats were immediately taken by two other players.

His luck continued for several more hours. Being more curious than ever about the amount of money that was stacked in front of him he set superstition aside and counted his chips. To his delight the amount was now $102,300. He knew it was time to shag his butt out of there and head for home free of the burden that he came with. Before he could declare that he was leaving he was dealt a hand. "What the hell," he thought "It didn't cost me any blinds, I'll take a look at my cards and muck them." To his surprise he saw a pair of aces, one a club and the other a heart. He was on the button (meaning in the dealer position) which is the best position at the table. Everyone mucked their cards in front of him leaving just the small and big blind behind him so he decided to slow play his aces and just call hoping one of them raises the bet. The small blind called the big blind and the big blind checked.

When the flop was turned over he could not believe his eyes; there before him was the ace of spade, ace of diamond and five of diamond. "Oh my God!" he thought to himself. "How much luck is too much luck for an individual in one day?" He suddenly remembered this happening to him in Baltimore.

Both players checked so Todd, not wanting to scare them

away, bet the minimum $200. The small blind mucked his hand but the big blind called. Fourth street presented a three of diamond. Still not wanting to scare off the remaining player he again bet the minimum of $200 in hopes he was chasing a flush or straight.

The big blind sat there pondering. "I should have checked," thought Todd, "He's not going to call and I'm going to win a small pot with this power hand, dammit!"

Suddenly he heard those two sweet words that he had been waiting for, 'all in'.

Todd looked to see how many chips the player had and was delighted to count $13,800. He quickly and proudly announced that he would call and threw up his two aces. "I got myself a good hand, four aces."

The other player looked over at Todd and smiled. "I don't think we ever introduced ourselves. I heard your name mentioned; Todd isn't it? My name is Butch Heintzel. You're one hell of a player my friend and one would think you have the nuts with four aces. If I were you I would have thought the same and called my all-in but you see there are times when pocket aces ain't all that and there are times, not many, but a few times, when four aces won't win."

Todd had about enough of Butch's small talk and abruptly told him to turn over his cards. "You can't beat my four aces friend so why prolong giving up your chips. Let's get on with the game. I know you got a flush and you were sadly mistaken when you figured me for a set."

With that same smile on his face, Butch replied, "You're right my friend I do have a flush and just a flush won't beat four of a kind but if you check the five up cards on the table you will notice there is an ace, five and three of diamond. These three cards fit ever so nicely with my two I'm holding." Butch threw down the two and four of diamonds giving him a straight flush.

Todd could not believe what he was seeing; it was a straight flush alright and just like that he was out over $14,000 of the money he so desperately needed.

He thought, "I could leave here with about $88,000 and still be in good shape but there is over $14,000 of my chips in front of Butch and I want them back"!

On bad beats some players go "on tilt" without realizing it and Todd was no exception. He pulled himself up close to the table and said in a determined voice, "Let's play some poker."

Several hours later and without realizing what was happening to him, Todd was down to $20,000 in chips and most of them were in front of Butch. He tried too hard to get his chips back but Butch tightened up and played conservative. There was no way he was giving back all that money to Todd.

As it happens so often the cards went cold for Todd. He folded when he shouldn't have and played when he had nothing. Earlier when he was catching belly buster straights and flushing on the river became quite the opposite now. Nothing was falling in his favor. At times when he did straighten or flush someone had something higher in rank.

His stomach was churning and sweat was beginning to form around his upper lip. It appeared that it was not likely he was going to do anything except go broke. Now down to his last $3,000 he humbly got up from the table and cashed in his chips.

Chapter Nine

Not knowing what time of day it was, nor did he care, Todd got in his car and started driving. The direction didn't matter to him just as long as the car kept moving. Several times the thought of suicide entered his mind. Each time the thought of destroying himself got stronger and stronger for he knew what would happen when he got home and was forced to tell Debbie the whole truth. Losing her and the children was a burden he could not cope with.

The truth however had to come out. She had to know about Skinnerbache and what he was capable of doing to her in order to send him a message. Getting his family out of harm's way would be, at the very least, the last decent thing he could do. After that he could decide what to do about himself. The decision was made, no matter what, this had to be done.

Several hours later he pulled in his driveway. Afraid of the consequences that would most certainly follow; he sat motionless in his car. The thought of having to tell his wife the whole truth turned him into jelly.

Suddenly there was a rap on the car window; it was Debbie. "Todd, are you alright"?

He was afraid to face her and continued to stare straight ahead. Once again she asked, "Are you alright"?

He slowly turned his head and looked into the eyes of the woman who loved and trusted him. He could no longer hold back his grief and immediately broke down crying like a small child.

With tears streaming down his cheeks, he said, "Oh honey! Please forgive me. I didn't mean for this to involve you and the children. Please, oh please forgive me."

He left nothing out of his confession to Deb. An hour later she knew everything and Todd could only hope she would somehow, in her heart, forgive him one more time.

It took a while for her to absorb all the shocking details of his confession. For what seemed an eternity to Todd and without a word she just stared at him. At times her eyes were cold as ice and other times he detected warmth and compassion.

Finally she said, "Todd, for sometime I felt there was something terribly wrong but I was afraid to ask. I really thought it was another woman. If only that was the case I would know how to handle it but this is something out of my league and obviously yours too. You accepted that money with no idea how it would be paid back and you put yourself and your family in jeopardy. You have a sickness Todd and there is no pill you can take that will cure this illness; you need to talk to a professional. Your children and wife now have to up-root themselves to avoid being hurt or even worse. We love you Todd but now I'm wondering if you really love us. Do you Todd? Do you?"

Unable to hold back any longer she broke down and began to cry. Todd tried to hold her but she pushed him away saying over and over again, "Don't touch me!"

He walked to the other side of the room and slumped down on the couch with his head in his hands.

Regaining her composure she walked over to where he was

sitting. Standing over him she said in a stern voice, "You've ruined our lives Todd! Do you realize that we will probably lose our home and our cars, everything! See what your addiction got you? I'm leaving Todd and I'm taking the kids. We're going to my parents in State College. I'll give you exactly one month to get this problem solved. If you do and you promise never to get involved in gambling ever again, then and only then, will I consider coming back, do you understand me?"

He removed his hands from in front of his face and looked up at her, "Thanks darling, I won't let you down. I'll have this problem resolved and be employed within thirty days, I promise you."

As his family pulled out of the driveway headed for State College he suddenly realized he had less than three weeks to raise the $65,000 to pay off Skinnerbache.

He wanted his family back just as soon as possible, realizing they were the most important thing in his life. Tomorrow was the day he would prioritize his life and get it back on track but tonight he would travel to Baltimore to see Chris.

Chapter Ten

Later that evening Todd tried calling Chris on his cell phone but all he got was his voice mail. He tried several times without success. Finally he gave up and decided to go out for a bite to eat at the local restaurant. He realized he forgot to take his cell phone with him but he would be sure to check it along with his home phone for any messages. He was also expecting to hear from Deb since he asked her to call when she arrived at her parents. There was one message on both phones. The one on the home phone was from his wife telling him they arrived okay. He immediately returned her call and they talked for about forty-five minutes. The other one was from Chris which he returned immediately after he hung up with Deb.

"The reason I called Chris was to find out if Skinnerbache was flexible with his clients if they are unable to payback their loans on time or in full.

There was a long pause at the other end and Todd said, "You still there Chris?"

Finally Chris spoke, "Man, don't tell me you can't pay this guy! If I knew you couldn't meet your loan I would have never taken you there. This guy is vicious! Todd, tell me this is not the case.

Skinnerbache will send his goons after you and if you avoid him your wife and kids will be next. His goons are sadistic bastards. I heard stories about them breaking arms and legs, even raping some guy's wife right in front of him."

"To tell you the truth," Todd replied, "I can't see how I can raise $65,000 in less than three weeks."

He could hear Chris taking several deep breaths. "Todd, my man, you are in deep crap and I don't have a rope to pull you out. What the hell are you going to do? He knows where you live and as sure as God made little green apples he'll come up there after you."

Todd bared his soul and told Chris everything, losing his job, having the money then losing it along with losing his family.

He held the phone away from his ear as Chris screamed, "What the hell is wrong with you, are you crazy?"

As the conversation continued Todd found out that one of Chris' friends also owed Skinnerbache over $5,000. He was unable to pay him back the following week as promised so the goons took a baseball bat to his car breaking all the windows, head lights and bashed in the hood. After the car they took the bat to his left leg fracturing it in two places. His friend is currently hiding out at Chris's apartment and that's the reason they did not answer the phone when Todd first called as they were screening all incoming calls. Luckily the guy's not married which gives him the freedom to move from one place to another in order to avoid Skinnerbach's goons. He didn't shown up at his job for several days so he is most likely fired but he figures that's a small price to pay because the next time they find him it will be much worse.

"God, he's worse off than I am," said Todd, "At least I have a little time in my favor. Is there any way you and your friend could drive up here tomorrow? We got to figure some way out of this for both of us. What's your friend's name?"

"His name is Jack Spoon but all his friends call him Spooney," replied Chris, "Yeah, there's no reason why we can't come up tomorrow. I don't have the $5,000 to loan him and I've been racking my brain trying to think of some way to help the guy."

Todd gave him directions to his house and told him around 2 p.m. would be a good time.

The following day around 1 p.m. Todd's phone rang. It was Chris at the other end, "Hey buddy were on I-83 just below the Mason/Dixon line. I just want to be sure I wrote down the right directions." And then there was nothing but silence.

Todd figured he hit a dead spot and waited for him to call him back. 2 p.m. came and went but there was no call from Chris. He tried calling him several times but got no answer. Finally the phone rang around 4:30 p.m. The voice at the other end was that of a shaken man. The trembling voice was Chris'. "Hey Todd you won't believe what I'm about to tell you. About a mile south of the Mason/Dixon a car ran us off the road. It was Skinnerbach's goonies. They grabbed Spooney and took him with them and warned me not to say anything or they would look me up. I don't know what the hell to do Todd! They got my friend and God knows what they will do to him." Todd could hear the hysteria mounting in his voice. "What shall I do man? I just can't let them hurt him anymore than they have, hell they might even kill him!"

Todd interrupted his friend, "Hey buddy, you got to call the Maryland State Police right away. Where are you calling from?"

Chris took a couple seconds to find a landmark, "Do you know where Leader's Heights is? I'm right off the exit."

"I know exactly where you are. Stay put and I'll be there as soon as I can but in the meantime call the Maryland State Police, don't hesitate another moment. It's the only way you can help your friend. We'll worry about Skinnerbache later. When the police arrive don't hold back, tell them everything."

Todd jumped in his car and flew down I-83 disregarding all the speed limits. When he got there he saw Chris talking with both Maryland and Pennsylvania State Police.

As he approached Chris and the officers he immediately identified himself.

I was surprised to find out that Chris already told them about my dealings with Skinnerbache.

When the Pennsylvania State Police found out the incident occurred in Maryland they quickly dismissed themselves and left but not before getting a statement from Todd. After a strong and lengthy lecture from them about borrowing money from a loan shark he was advised to get the money together and pay Skinnerbache off before something bad happened to him. He couldn't have agreed more.

Chris gave his cell number and Todd's home and cell numbers to the police in case they had to contact him.

When the state police left the two friends stopped in a bar across the street to calm their nerves with a drink or two. Shortly after, they left for home with Todd leading the way and Chris following in his car.

Chapter Eleven

The day after the kidnapping Chris got a call from the police. Spooney was a patient at one of the local hospitals with the other leg and two fingers of his left hand broken. When questioned he told them he fell while trying to climb the stairs of his apartment building without his crutches. He denied owing money to, or even knowing, Skinnerbache and said he was not abducted by anyone the day before. When asked how he got to the hospital he told them one of his friends drove him there. When checking out his story they found he couldn't remember his friend's name. It was obvious he was lying to protect himself. This being the case no charges could be filed against Skinnerbache.

Chris was now deeply concerned about returning to Baltimore for fear the goons would put the fear of God in him and break one of his limbs in order to keep him quiet.

Todd noticed his concern and suggested he stay at his house until things calmed down, after all, there was plenty of room now that Deb and the kids left. Chris quickly accepted his kind offer.

Two weeks went by very fast. During that time neither one could come up with a solution to Todd's problem nor could he find a job suitable to his abilities. He made the statement that he would be damned if he would flip burgers at a fast food joint or work on a production line in a factory. Due to the fact that a large manufacturing plant moved out of the county, unemployment was at its all time high so even if it got down to flipping burgers or a factory job there wouldn't be an opening.

The $3,000 he had several weeks ago was now more than half gone. He had to pay the mortgage of $1,100 plus all the utilities and then came a notice in the mail from the bank demanding a $350 past due payment on the car.

Seeing the situation Todd was in, Chris suggested they take a late night trip to his place where he had $1,500 stashed away. The later they went the better the odds of avoiding Skinnerbache so around midnight they were on their way south on I-83.

Taking the long way around took about thirty minutes longer but they arrived without any problems. Chris immediately retrieved the cash and stuffed it in his pocket. He asked Todd if he would like a drink and relax before they headed back. This seemed like the right thing to do and Todd obliged him. Before realizing it they consumed a half bottle of scotch. They decided to stay put for awhile knowing neither one was sober enough to drive. The last thing they wanted was to be detained in Baltimore facing a DUI charge. Todd fell asleep on the couch and Chris stretched out on top of his bed.

Suddenly Todd awoke and noticed it was after nine in the morning. He immediately shook Chris awake telling him get himself ready for a quick departure.

Chris, being more adventuresome than Todd, suggested that since they were already getting a late start why not find out what hospital Spooney was in and stop by to make sure he was okay.

Not thinking this was such a brilliant idea, Todd suggested they head on back to Pennsylvania and visit his friend another time.

Chris, having a persistent and persuasive nature, convinced him there was nothing to worry about. He reminded Todd that he still had a couple days left before his $65,000 was due.

It was not what Todd felt in his gut to do but reluctantly agreed to, providing it was a short visit.

It took several phone calls to various hospitals only to find out that Spooney had been released sometime ago without a forwarding address. That was understandable due to the circumstances. He made a call to his friend's mother and found out he was with his father in Westminster, Maryland. His mother and father had been divorced for sometime.

With that done and Chris satisfied, they headed north for Pennsylvania and home. There they would have only a few short days to come up with some plan to avoid any injury to Todd.

As they pulled into the driveway Todd sensed something was not right. The front porch lights were out. It was always the practice of his family to turn the lights on, day or night, when any of them left the house. The second thing he noticed was a late model black Cadillac parked by the corner of the street. No one on his street owned a black Cadillac to his knowledge. It didn't dawn on him at the time to check the license plate.

He made Chris aware of his uneasiness but his friend though nothing of it. "You're starting to get the jitters ole buddy. You got two whole days to come up with some ideas and maybe another two until they get around to you so relax."

"I guess you're right," replied Todd, "With all that's been happening I probably forgot to turn on the lights when we left yesterday."

Thinking about what Chris said eased his mind and he proceeded to sort out the house key from his key ring and opened the front door. When they entered the foyer and walked into the living room they froze in their tracks. Sitting there was two of

Skinnerbache's henchmen. The one black dude stood up and walked over to where they were standing. He stood within inches of them, towering over the two like a red wood tree in an effort to intimidate. It obviously worked, for as both of them tried to take a step back but were grabbed by their shirts and pulled even closer to his ugly face.

Speaking in a graveled voice one could immediately tell he was as educated as a slug on the sidewalk after a summer shower. His diction and pronunciation of words were so bad you had to decipher what he was saying. When he was finished talking Todd looked at Chris with an expression on his face that seemed to say, "What the hell did he just say"?

As Chris looked up at the goon he said, "Did you just say that you knew we were in Baltimore and came up here yesterday to find us and that you were taking us back to see your boss"?

"Das right," was the only answer Chris got.

Todd got up enough courage to ask how they got into his house and the other goon spoke up. By putting every third intelligible word or so together he thought he said, "There wasn't a back door around that could not be opened."

Todd and Chris were now on their way back to Baltimore in the back of the black Cadillac. Not knowing what to expect they could only suspect that it had something to do with Spooney's disappearance. As fast as this car was moving they would soon find out. Todd estimated they were traveling 75 to 80 miles per hour which is way over the speed limit. They could only hope that they would be pulled over by a cop and get out of this situation but that didn't happen. With a concerned smile Chris looked over at Todd and said, "Where is a cop when you need one?"

Sooner than they realized, the car pulled up in front of Skinnerbache's building. The car door was opened and they were hustled inside and made to stand in front of the loan shark's unoccupied desk. They probably stood there a good five minutes before Skinnerbache limped in with a cane in hand and sat down. It appeared very painful, probably from some sort of injury or a bad case of gout.

He sat there motionless and stared at Chris. It seemed like an eternity before he spoke. Finally he said, "Chris, I'm going to ask you this just once and once only. Where are you hiding Mr. Spoon?"

As he stood there he began to squirm. He rocked back and forth, first on one foot then the other. Thinking before he answered, he replied, "Well, to be very honest, I don't know where he's at. I haven't seen him since the I-83 incident.

Before he could finish saying what he wanted to, one of tough guys walked over and struck him between the shoulder blades with his large fist.

Chris crumpled to the floor like a rag doll writhing in pain. As soon as he hit the floor he was immediately picked up and made to stand on his feet again.

In a calm but business like manner Skinnerbache said, "Now Mr. Chris, do you want to rephrase your statement or should I have one of my men help you refresh your memory?"

Chris was now standing in a slumped position as though he was bowing to royalty. Unable to speak but one or two words at a time he said, "Yes, I know where Spooney is. I know the town but not the address and that's all I know. I'm sure if you knew the town you could find him easily enough. What are you going to do to him that you already haven't done? What bones are left for you to break? You incapacitated him now to where he can't hold down a job to earn enough money to pay you back even if he wanted to. What's the point in that? Is this the way you get your kicks in life you bastard!"

Out of the corner of Todd's eye he could see one goon walking toward Chris. His fists were clenched and ready to do more harm to him.

Chris bent over lower, reached down and pulled a small hand gun from the top of his boot. He quickly cocked the hammer and pointed it at the oncoming tough guy. It appeared to be a small caliper gun, much like a Derringer. In a shaky but determined voice, Chris said, "You come one more step toward me you big son-of-a-bitch and you'll walk right into a piece of flying lead. You're used to passing out pain, how would you like to experience some yourself?" He then alternated his aim back and forth between the henchman and Skinnerbache. "How about you Mr. loan shark, would you like a slug in that bad food of yours?"

Skinnerbache stood up and limped two or three steps back from his desk. "Chris, if you put that gun away and stop pointing it at me both of you can leave without any problem; in fact, we'll give you the keys to the car you came in."

As soon as the car key offer was made they came sliding across the hardwood floor and stopped a few feet from Todd. With caution he leaned over and picked them up.

Chris was hurting real bad but managed to keep himself together. Continuing to dart his gun from one to the other and with an intent look in his eyes he said, "We would have gotten the keys anyway and this gun guarantees that we will walk out of here so your offer, big guy, ain't worth a pile of cow dung. Further more; I'm hurting like crazy because you, Mr. loan shark, ordered your bad boys to beat up on me. That's got to be worth some sort of payback. Don't you think?"

Hearing these threatening words startled Skinnerbache. In an effort to get away he somehow tripped over his cane and fell forward striking his head on the corner of the desk.

Todd looked at Chris and began to shake. "Hey man, this guy isn't moving; he looks like he's dead!"

Chris, still in pain pointed his gun at the other tough guy and said, "Hey dumb ass, get over there and check out your boss."

Very cautiously and not moving his eyes from the gun the man slowly approached his boss and kneeled down to check him out. "He ain't breathing man, I think he's dead."

Chris's demeanor suddenly changed from bad to worse. He became more aggressive and began to talk very loud. "Get your ass over there and stand next to your dumb friend. Move it!"

The goon immediately got to his feet and walked quickly to the side of his partner. They both stood there not knowing what to expect next.

With gun in hand, Chris walked dangerously close to them and smiled. It was a crazed smile, not like one would smile when walking by another in the aisle of a super market. Looking them in the eye he blurted out angrily, "Now that your boss is dead what do you think I should do with you guys? With what you did to Spooney a while back and what you did to me tonight I have some great ideas."

Before he could utter another word the one guy blurted out, "Hey man don't you get any crazy ideas! Just stay cool, alright?" Hey man, take the car and leave. We didn't see anything, we don't know anything. As a matter of fact we don't even know you. Look here, I know where Mr. Skinnerbache keeps all his information on both of you. Suppose I get them for you and no one will ever know either one of you ever did any business with him. If I do that for you will you let us go?"

"Get the damn information and I'll think about it," replied Chris.

Not trusting either one of them, Chris made both of them walk together to the next room where there was a metal file cabinet setting in the corner. With a demanding tone to his voice he ordered them to open it.

Chris made them step aside and motioned Todd to get all their files, including Spooney's.

Now that they had the files, the one guy nervously asked if Chris was going to let them go.

With that crazed look on his face he reminded them he would be carrying his gun on him at all times and would not hesitate to use it. He went even further to say if he or his two friends had a simple accident like tripping over a rake handle while working in their yard he would come looking for them.

"Don't worry about us," replied one of the goons, "We've been talking about moving to Las Vegas and I think you just made up our minds."

"My-o-my," chuckled Chris, "It's amazing how well you can speak with a gun in your face."

Backing away slowly the two exited the building and sped off in the black Cadillac. They drove to the Inner Harbor where Chris called Tom (one of the players at O.B.'s games) and asked him to drive them back to Pennsylvania. Being the good hearted guy that he was he said he would. He only asked one question and that was how they got to the Inner Harbor without a car. Chris didn't want to queer the chance of getting transportation back to Todd's house so he told him his car broke down and was being towed to the garage. Tom told him it would be around an hour before he could get there.

While waiting for their ride the two thought it wise to wipe the car clean of fingerprints front and back. It wouldn't be sitting there too long before the police checked it out.

As they were cleaning up the car Todd asked Chris if he got wild and wooly often like he did with the two heavy weights back at Skinnerbache's place.

He answered with a chuckle, "Hell no Todd, I studied acting a few years back hoping I could make it a career but things didn't work out. I was scared out of my wits playing that scene. The gun I have isn't even real. It's a prop I kept from one of the tryouts."

The following morning Todd woke up with a much better outlook. Since Skinnerbache was dead and his two goons heading for Las Vegas, he now could concentrate on finding a good job and getting his family back.

Chris decided to drive to Westminster and see how Spooney was doing. From there he would head on home to Baltimore.

Chapter Twelve

For the next few days Todd checked the help wanted ads in the newspaper and on the internet. He managed to get two interviews but was turned down on both. He figured his previous employer had a lot to do with it but he would keep trying no matter what for he knew it was the only way to get his family back.

He kept in contact with Deb and continuously asked her to come home but she refused until he was once again financially stable.

He continued his quest for employment but after several weeks finally came to the conclusion his career in sales/ management was over. He had no alternative but to step down to a lesser paying job but even they were scarce and the pay they offered could never support the life style his family was used to.

Once again time was against him and his finances were critical. The mortgage was due very soon and the car payments for both autos were in default. He had barely enough ready cash to last more than a week or ten days.

He thought that when the $65,000 problem was over and done with, it would be downhill for him but without acquiring a job immediately his chances of keeping his home and cars were next to none let alone getting his family back. He felt everything closing in on him what with the creditors' overdue notices in the mail and the threatening phone calls; something had to be done soon and he realized it. Thinking back on how he squandered his money on poker and the stupid move he made at the company he was fired from made him sick to the stomach.

As he sat there in his favorite lounge chair contemplating what to do the following day he was startled by the loud ring of the phone. He hesitated picking up the receiver for fear that it may be another creditor calling. Before doing so he checked the caller ID and found it was Chris calling from Maryland.

The news he got from Chris was not of interest to him. It was about a big Texas hold-em tournament that was being held two weeks from now in the small town of Glen Rock, PA, just down the road from where Todd lives. He got this information from Wendy, the dealer at O.B.'s games; she was chosen to be one of the dealers. The place and time is being kept secret to avoid any possible problems; only those invited to play will know about it. There will be 100 invitations with a $10,000 entry which means the winner could walk away with literally hundreds of thousands of dollars.

Todd was just about to tell him he was not the least bit interested when suddenly a thought popped in his head. He asked Chris if he and Spooney could come up to his place. Chris asked him when and Todd told him the sooner the better. They decided sooner was better and planned to meet that very evening.

While waiting for the guys to show up Todd checked his e-mails and found he got replies from two of his résumé's he submitted earlier. The first one thanked him for his time but said the job had been filled. The second one gave him their phone number and asked him to call them as soon as possible.

With hope in his heart he immediately placed the call and was connected to the human relations department. He was told he had exactly the background and experience they were looking for but when they checked his previous employer they did not receive a favorable recommendation. Realizing that it is not always the employee's fault for being terminated they told him if he could contact his previous employer and clear it up they would strongly consider him for the job.

His heart sank as he hung up the phone for he knew it would be impossible to convince his old boss Tony to help him out but he had no alternative but to at least try.

With his heart on his sleeve and hat in hand he picked up the phone and called him. It was one of the hardest things he ever had to do but he knew he had to at least give it a try, even if it meant begging.

He spoke with Tony for nearly half an hour but to no avail. Tony stood his ground and said in good conscience he could not recommend him.

All his hopes of obtaining a suitable job were shattered. The only thing left now was his plan for the upcoming Texas hold-em tournament. He could only hope Chris and Spooney would go along with his crazy idea.

Later that day the two arrived from Baltimore. Although on crutches, Spooney moved around pretty well.

As they were having a drink Todd told them he was about to lose everything very soon unless he came up with some money.

Thinking Todd was about to ask him for a loan Chris spoke up telling him he was tapped out. Of course Spooney didn't have to say anything for everyone knew he was broke and without a job.

"That's the point I'm trying to make to both of you," replied Todd, "The three of us are in dire need of ready cash. Now how do you suppose we could lay our hands on some of it? We could rob a bank of course but with today's technologies such as high tech cameras and computers we would most likely be caught before we could spend one dime of it. Where would hundreds of thousands of dollars or maybe a million be without the protection of sophisticated equipment around to insure its safety? I'd say nowhere, absolutely nowhere, except for one place. Is there anyone in this room that would like to venture a guess?"

Chris rose from the couch and pointed his finger at Todd. "Are you suggesting we knock off the Texas hold-em tournament that's coming up?"

Todd smiled and pointed his finger back at Chris. "You got a better idea?"

Chris began laughing out loud. "You know what Todd; you are a crazy sick son-of-a-bitch to think we could get away with a hair-brained idea like that. What the hell are you thinking of? That's the most stupid idea I ever heard but you know it's so crazy and so stupid it might work. Count me in."

Spooney made an attempt to get to his feet but lost his balance and fell back down on the couch. "Hey, you're counting me in on this aren't you?"

Todd patted him on his head and replied, "Hell yes, you're going to be our main man."

The three of them were now a team. All they had to do now was to devise a foolproof plan. It had to be a plan that would go off without a hitch or they would be facing serious consequences.

It was decided that since Spooney was incapacitated due to his injuries he would be the straight guy. This meant he would have to be a player at the table, an inside guy, if you will. Question now was how to get him invited to the game and where was the $10,000 coming from.

While pondering these two questions they decided to drive to the Pizza Hut for pizza and beer. As they were sipping on beer and waiting for their pizza to be served, Todd asked if they knew how many bundles of money would make $10,000 of cash.

Chris was sure if they were hundred dollar bills it would be two bundles of $5,000 each.

Todd then asked if the three of them could get four authentic $100 bills together by game time. Todd already had two of them tucked away in his wallet for emergency purposes and agreed to donate them if the other two could spring for one each. They saw no problem in that and promised to have them to Todd at least two days before the game started.

After their fill of pizza and beer the three went back to the house to further discuss their plans. Their caper had to be flawless because just one slip-up could mean spending time in jail and that is something none of them wanted.

There were several obstacles that had to be overcome. Spooney would be working on the inside as a player but in order for this to work they would need a second inside person. That person would have to be the one taking the entry fee from the players as they enter the room. All three agreed if they could find out who it would be and they were trustworthy they would offer a $50,000 piece of the pie.

Since Wendy first told Chris about the game he said he would contact her to see if she knew who it would be.

Todd suggested that Chris get as much information from Wendy as he could without raising suspicion. One very important piece of information they needed was a list of names attending the game. Without the names it might be necessary to enlist the help of two more people which would mean shelling out another $100,000.

Spooney asked how all the players were going to allow someone to just walk out with their money.

Chris smiled and said, "Spooney that is one part of the plan you will not be told about for we want that to be as much of a surprise as everyone else in the room."

It was getting late so Chris and Spooney headed back to Baltimore.

The following morning around 10 a.m. Todd was on the phone with Deb when the call waiting beeped. He asked his wife to hold for a minute and pushed the flash button; it was Chris and he was excited. Todd quickly switched back to his wife to tell her he would call her back.

Chris told him they hit pay dirt, "You won't believe the news I got for you. Spooney and I will be there around noon time and we're bringing Wendy with us. Trust me, its okay for her to come. That's all I'm saying right now so have some lunch for us when we arrive.

At 11:30 a.m. they arrived with Wendy. Todd greeted her with a hand shake and guided them to the dining room for soup and sandwiches.

It was very noticeable that Wendy looked much better than the last time Todd saw her at O.B."s place. He complimented her on how nice she looked as he pulled the chair from the table for her to sit down.

Very little if anything was discussed regarding their caper during lunch but when everyone was finished and the second cup of coffee was poured Chris opened the meeting. "Todd, I told you on the phone I had some great news for you. Yesterday when I got home I gave Wendy a call and she was quite willing to meet with me at 8:00 this morning. After the first fifteen minutes she quickly figured out I had something in mind other than getting an invitation to the game. Without hesitation she told me that all the information she had was mine as long as there was something in it for her. I told her there would be $50,000 if she agreed to do what we ask. I assured her there was little or no risk in her involvement. Hearing that she told me she had the list of players that would be attending but so far there are only eighty-six confirmed returns of the one hundred invited. As far as Spooney getting on the list she could see no problem if there are no-shows which would be a wait and see situation. The other bit of information you need is the time, date and place. Wendy tells me it will be two weeks from this Sunday at three p.m. The owner of one of the largest lumber companies in Baltimore is hosting it at his home in Glen Rock. His home is huge consisting of two game rooms. He already has two game tables of his own and is renting eight more to accommodate the tournament."

Todd was glad to hear Chris' report but now wanted to hear from Wendy. He asked her why she wanted to get involved in something like this.

Wendy took a sip of her coffee and paused for a moment before answering. "There are two reasons why I want to take the chance, well maybe three, but the main reason is that a while back I had some serious medical problems and the insurance my husband had only covered part of it which left me with a healthy balance of over $25,000. My husband passed away about three months ago with a heart attack and I have no way of coming up with the money unless I sell my home and that would break my heart. My second reason is I work for the bastard that is having this tournament. He treats his employees, which includes me, like dirt. No one has any respect for him so this would be my small way of giving him a punch in that fat belly of his. And thirdly, from what Chris told me I have very little risk. Who's going to suspect little old me?"

Spooney asked her what the chances were of getting him on the list.

"I'll place you in the number one spot of the alternate list and you will be the first one picked if someone doesn't show but I highly suggest you use a name other than your own; I notice you are on crutches which gives me an idea. Would you like to be the flamboyant son of very rich financier from California? A reckless playboy who loves racing cars and recently rushed to the hospital due to a pile up on the far turn? I think that suits you perfectly. Your name is, let's see, how about Fast Freddie Ford. That has a ring to it. If there should happen to be race fans at the game they won't necessarily have to know of you because you never raced big time due to your recklessness. I think that would be perfect, don't you?'

Her idea was accepted with enthusiasm and would definitely be incorporated into their plans.

Wendy then asked why it was necessary for Spooney to be a player and Todd spoke up telling her it was very necessary for he and Chris to know exactly when to make their move. "When everyone is seated and into the game, Spooney will call us on his cell phone letting it ring just one time which will be our cue."

So far all the loose ends were tied up, all except one, the guarantee of getting Spooney inside. Being on the waiting list was just not good enough; it had to be a rock solid guarantee.

Everyone went over the invitational list several times but found no one they knew, which was good. The names consisted of judges, politicians, big time lawyers, several car dealers and many business owners. Just as Wendy was about to pick it up and put it in her pocketbook Spooney grabbed it. "Hey, wait a minute, look at this." He pointed at two names. "Do you see what I see? There are two names from out of town, one from Scranton, PA and the other from Denver, Colorado."

Chris picked up the list and studied the two names. "What's your point Spooney, you know them?"

"No, No, I don't know them even though the guys name from Denver does look familiar. Didn't he use to play for the Broncos?

My point is that both will be traveling. The guy from Scranton will probably drive his car and the guy from Denver will most likely fly to BWI then rent a car and drive to Glen Rock. Now if one of them fails to show up for one reason or the other, such as getting lost or maybe their car breaks down I would get their spot at the table."

With the wheels now in motion they decided to end their meeting for now. To avoid any suspicion it was agreed that Wendy not attend any future get-togethers. When necessary, Chris or Spooney would personally contact her. There would be no phone calls to or from her.

Once again Spooney came up with a great idea. He suggested going to a place like Wal-Mart and buying a kid's walkie-talkie set to communicate with her. They could sit in their cars a block away from each other and transmit information back and forth.

Prior to heading back to Baltimore, Todd asked if either one had any information on Skinnerbache. Chris said he had been checking the obituaries on a daily basis but found nothing. Wondering if he was still alive was not something they wanted to worry about especially at this time. The three of them would never feel safe until they knew for sure so Chris decided to pose as one of his relatives and call the various hospitals in the area.

The following morning he picked the hospital nearest Skinnerbache's residence assuming that would be the one the emergency medical team would rush him to if he was alive. After several minutes of waiting on the phone he got the news. Skinnerbache had been an overnight patient in their emergency room but was released the following day. He thought if he told Todd about this it would weigh on his mind and screw things up so he decided not to say anything until they finished the job

With several more days of air tight planning they would be ready. To be ready is one thing but to pull it off without any major problems would be another.

Chapter Thirteen

Chris spoke with Wendy several times on the walkie-talkie and with the information she gave them they decided to delay the guy flying in from Denver rather than the Scranton player. According to Wendy the guy from Scranton has a friend that knows the Denver player and recommended him. Some of the other players knew the Scranton player but no one knew the guy coming from Denver so he was the obvious choice.

The eventful day finally came. Todd drove to Baltimore to meet with Chris and Spooney. There was one last bit of information they needed so they drove by Wendy's residence and contacted her on the walkie-talkie. Wendy had the information they needed on the Denver player, Southwest Airlines flight number 341 arriving at BWI at 10:05 a.m. This gave Chris and Todd a little less than an hour to get there so the prepared to leave for BWI immediately.

To round out his masquerade as a flamboyant playboy Spooney rented a flashy sports car to drive to Glen Rock. This final touch caused him to max out his credit card.

With the four one hundred dollar bills they gave her, Wendy found a green paper that nearly matched the color of money and cut down several reams of it to make two bundles then placed a real bill on the top and bottom of each bundle. Before giving them to Spooney she wrapped each bundle with several wide rubber bands making them appear authentic. Before leaving for the game she made sure Spooney's fictitious name was added to the list of players. Her time of departure was twelve noon to assure being there one hour before the 2 p.m. starting time. It was her job to check off the players name and collect their $10,000 and then be ready to deal the cards at one of the tables.

Todd and Chris arrived at BWI in plenty of time. They were fortunate that the traffic was unusually light for that time of day. The plan was to pose as two of the players there to pick him up then drive to Holtwood Dam and drop him off by the river where he would have to walk for several miles to civilization. This would give them time to rush back to Glen Rock and finish the job before anyone was the wiser. They had no reason to be worried about him identifying them but to be safe both of them wore wigs with a mustache and sun glasses. Along with his quest to be an actor, Chris at one time worked behind stage as a make-up man. With his past experience he did a great job making everything look quite natural. They had a placard with the name John Bourne printed on it and would merely wait until he recognized his name and walked up to them.

It would be a good ten minutes until the arrival of his flight so the two relaxed in the lounge until his flight number was announced.

A few minutes after they sat down Todd's cell phone rang. He noticed it was his parent's calling. "Hello dad is that you?"

"Yes son it's me. I got a very strange visitor just a while ago; it was a big scary black guy. He said he knows you and asked how he could get in touch with you. Of course I didn't give him any information; are you in trouble son?"

"No dad don't worry, it's about a job I've been after. He's the chauffer of the guy that owns the company where I applied for a job; give me his number."

"Ok son I was a little worried there for a while. The number is 401-555-1514, good luck."

Chris could see the blood drain from Todd's face as he shut off his cell phone. "What's wrong? Something happen to your dad or mom?"

It took a minute for Todd to pull himself together, finally he spoke.

They both knew who the big black guy was. It was one of Skinnerbache's henchmen.

Chris knew it was now time to come clean with what he knew about Skinnerbache's release from the hospital.

Todd tried to understand his reasoning but was still upset about him withholding this kind of information.

With hesitation Todd dialed the number. The voice at the other end was Skinnerbache's. "Well, well Mr. Todd did you really think you were free and clear of the money you owe me? As a matter of fact the $65,000 has grown in interest to, oh let me see now, I think its $100,000. Pay me you son-of-a-bitch or you'll never see you wife or kids ever again! Oh, and by the way you could never guess where the boys are driving me to as we speak. I'll save you the trouble; we're on our way to a town called State College and were not going there to see a football game. I understand from what your father said your family is there for a visit, right? I think we'll stop by to say hello and maybe she'll invite us to dinner. Yeah, I think that's a capital idea. We might even hang out there for a couple hours and maybe you would like to come up and join the party."

Afraid for his family's safety Todd pleaded with Skinnerbache. "I swear to God I'll have the money to you this very day if you give me the chance but I won't be able to get my hands on it until later this evening."

"How are you going to lay your hands on $100,000 in such a short time, rob a bank? Look, I don't give a rat's ass how you get it, that's your business, but there's only one way I'll go along with it and here's the deal. If it doesn't suit your fancy that's tough but it's all up to you because I'm finished negotiating. We'll stop at the Holiday Inn in Harrisburg and wait two hours for you. If you don't show up with the money we're heading for State College."

Todd was sweating by this time. He could see his world crumbling before him. It didn't seem fair for him to be so close to getting back to a normal life and then having it yanked out from under him. He made one last attempt to stall him until after the game. "But I won't have the money by then don't you understand? It will be later in the afternoon or early evening until I can get it."

Skinnerbache claimed he knew all the tricks of the trade. He quickly surmised that Todd would use this time to go to State College and take off with his family so he told him he would wait until early evening with one condition and that was for him to immediately come to Harrisburg and be their guest until he had someone else deliver the money.

Todd paused for several seconds trying desperately to think of something. "Is it okay if I call you back in a few minutes?"

"You got exactly three minutes, not a second more," replied Skinnerbache, "If we don't hear from you by then we are driving on to State College."

Barely managing to speak he told Chris about his conversation with Skinnerbache.

Chris knew the life or death situation his friend was in so he tried to stay calm and collected for his sake.

He knew very well that Todd was putting his life as well as his family's in his hands when he asked if he could pull this off alone and bring the money to Harrisburg.

Without hesitation Chris told him not to worry about a thing and to get his butt on the road to Harrisburg.

Chris being the only one able to think with a clear head suggested that Todd rent a car rather than use the one they came in. They wanted no evidence that Chris was ever here. He would be the only one that John Bourne could possibly recognize and he didn't want any record showing that he was anywhere near BWI. Even if they picked up on Todd's rental it would be of no consequence.

As Todd was leaving they were announcing the arrival of the Denver flight. Chris was concerned about his friend's concentration while driving in the heavy traffic. "Hey pal everything is going to work out just fine now stay alert on the highway and get there in one piece. You won't do your family any good if you get into an accident."

Todd promised him he would drive carefully and apologized for not being able to help him.

"Don't worry about it big guy. I was thinking earlier how we could use you somewhere else rather than here but didn't say anything since you were sure it was a two man job. Get going, you're wasting time and I got to get across the terminal. Wish me luck."

He stood there momentarily as Todd exited the building. As soon as he was out of sight he began to doubt himself. The plan that he and Todd devised was out the window and now it had to be played by ear. As he walked briskly across the terminal his head began to spin. "How is the best way to pull this off? What if this guy suspects foul play right from the start?"

Suddenly he heard a voice behind him. "Are you looking for me sir?"

Chris turned around and stared into the chest of one of the biggest men he ever stood next to. He had to be around 6' 9" to 7' and a good guess of his weight would be 350 pounds or more.

Looking up Chris asked if he was John Bourne and he said that he was. "I walked past you and saw my name on the card you were carrying. Apparently you were thinking of something else and didn't notice me pointing at you."

Surprisingly Chris collected himself and calmly replied, "Why yes, I guess I was spacing out a little, I just got here and thought I had missed you. I was designated to pick you up and take you to the game. You were told Glen Rock but the game has been moved to Annapolis which is just south of here. They discovered that there wasn't enough room at the other place to accommodate 100 players. They changed it just a few hours ago and there wasn't time to contact you since you were already on the plane heading east so I'll be your chauffer for the balance of the trip."

It seemed like an eternity before the Denver player said anything which made Chris' knees a little weak. All he could think of was how much it was going to hurt when he picked himself up off the floor with a face full of knuckles and several broken teeth.

Finally he spoke, "Well now, this is mighty nice of you to do this for me. Sure enough I would have been a lost puppy in this neck of the woods until I found the new address. Probably would have been eaten up in blinds until I found the game. Thank you very much!"

Chris quickly came to the conclusion that this guy was a big pussy cat. He probably wouldn't hurt a fly if it was crawling up his nose. He now became more confident that the situation at hand could be handled without incident but he momentarily had no clue of how he was going to dump this Neanderthal.

They gathered his luggage and put them in the trunk of the car and headed down the road. On the way John mentioned that he wired his buddy in Scranton his $10,000 for he felt uneasy carrying that much cash on the plane. This was good news to Chris since they figured that was money that would never reach the game.

The original plan was to be no further away from Glen Rock than two hours driving time. Since it was getting close to 11 a.m. he had to think of something quick. He mentioned to John that he was getting a little hungry and would like to stop off at the next restaurant for a bite to eat and John readily agreed. Of course it was obvious that the big guy never turned down a meal in his life.

While waiting to be served Chris asked John if he could borrow his cell phone. He asked this just to find out if he really had one. If he did it he could call his Scranton buddy and that would be disastrous. It could foil their whole plan and someone would definitely get hurt.

He was relieved to find out that John never carried one. He said he was forever getting calls from friends during one of these tournaments and all it did was break his concentration.

He then asked if he knew his Scranton buddy's cell phone number and was surprised to find out that he didn't. He told Chris he always called his home number but that was written down in a book back in his apartment in Denver.

Chris couldn't imagine this being any better. The man doesn't have a cell phone with him and depended entirely on his book at home for numbers. From all indications he was not the sharpest knife in the drawer. It would take him a long while to figure things out and much longer to even find his way back to BWI let alone the site of the game. Even if he was sure he was bamboozled would he take the chance of going to Glen Rock?

Their order was served and John, not having much to eat since early morning, dug right in.

Chris sipped his coffee and casually mentioned that he was going outside to make a call on his phone and gas up the car.

John noticed that Chris left his sandwich untouched and asked him if he was going to eat it. "Go ahead and eat it," replied Chris, "I'm really not that hungry. Take your time, I'm going to gas up the car and make my call while I'm out there."

The gas pumps were on the opposite side of the building and out of the sight of John which again, was more than a perfect situation. Chris pulled the car around the building and stopped the car. He opened the trunk and removed John's luggage and sat them neatly by the bushes but not before he slipped the gas attendant a ten dollar bill telling him to be sure the big guy in the restaurant gets them when he comes out.

He was running right on schedule but he couldn't waste any time getting back to Pennsylvania. The last thing he wanted was to be pulled over for a speeding violation.   As he was driving he suddenly remembered, not only did he leave big John stranded in 'nowheresville', he stuck him with the lunch check and tip.

Meanwhile Todd was on his way north on Interstate 83. As he was approaching Harrisburg he couldn't remember if Skinnerbache gave him the Holiday Inn address and room number so he redialed his number and got the information.

Ten minutes later he pulled into the motel parking lot and shut off the motor. He was more than a little nervous so he sat there trying to calm himself. Todd knew it was risky what he was doing but it was no longer about him it was his family that was now involved. If this was his last day on earth he would die knowing his loved ones would be safe.

He looked back over the past two years and thought how stupid he was to get himself in a mess like this and vowed to God that if he could see him safely through this ordeal he would be a good son, a wonderful husband and a great father. He was suddenly startled by the ringing of his cell phone. He was relieved to see it was Chris calling to find out if he made it to Harrisburg okay. Chris tried to reassure him that everything would turn out fine and not to worry. Before he hung up Chris got the directions to the motel and Skinnerbache's room number.

Todd mustered enough courage to exit his car and walk to room 117. He was about to knock on the door when it opened. He came face to face with one of the black guys that promised him and Chris that they moving to Las Vegas. The guy motioned him in without saying a word and pointed to a chair. As he walked to the chair Todd quickly noticed that there was no one else in the room except the two of them so he asked the whereabouts of Skinnerbache. He was told that he and the other big guy went looking for someone that owed money. After that they were going to dinner and would return in a couple hours.

Chapter Fourteen

It was now ten minutes until two and Chris was entering the town of Glen Rock. As he pulled onto the road where the game was being held he noticed a lot of cars parked in the driveway and along the road indicating that most everyone was there. As he was looking for an inconspicuous place to park his car he noticed a cherry red Corvette convertible. This had to be the car Spooney rented for the occasion.

Although he didn't say anything to Todd, Chris knew that the plan they worked so hard on was out the window. He had to come up with another one, one that would involve just himself. In just a few hours Spooney and Wendy would be expecting Todd and Chris to enter the poker room with a plan known only to the two of them.

He questioned whether to phone Spooney on his cell phone and advise him of the situation but he knew his phone was programmed to vibrate rather than ring and he might take it as the pre-planned signal that he and Todd were coming in and not answer it, Realizing this might screw things up he decided against it. He knew that for Todd and his family's sake there was no backing out so he had to think of something very soon. This was not a three person job; it had to be four to work smoothly.

It occurred to him to phone his friend Tom and let him in on the deal. He knew he could trust him but being married with kids he would probably decline. Even if he would take the chance it would take too much time for him to drive from Baltimore to Glen Rock.

And what about the Denver guy, John Bourne? Certainly by now he figured out that he was scammed and he wasn't too stupid to start asking directions to Glen Rock. What was to stop him from renting a car and driving here? He might be driving north on Interstate 83 this very moment. Chris had to think of something and act upon it in the next ninety minutes. He suddenly realized that if the plan fell through it could mean trouble for Spooney and Wendy as well, thus adding more pressure. This was becoming an unbearable situation knowing he was responsible for all these people. His guts were tying themselves in knots thinking about it.

Suddenly his phone rang. He was getting a call from Todd. Speaking very softly but very hurried, Todd said, "Hey Chris, I realize you are in one hell of a tight spot without me there with you and I want you to know that I will always be in your debt for doing this for me. I also know it's impossible for you to do this by yourself. There's someone on their way to help you and he should be there in the next hour or so. Hang tight until he gets there. Don't worry, he'll find you; he knows the car you're driving, stay put until he gets there. I'm here by myself but I don't know for how long. I'll explain everything later." Suddenly he began to speak very fast and whispered, "I got to go, someone's at the door."

Before Chris could say a word he hung up and there was complete silence. He knew it was Todd for he recognized his voice. He could not think of any reason this would be a set-up for a bust but to be sure he dialed Todd back. The phone rang six times and then his voice mail kicked in. This was very puzzling but he had to believe in his friend.

All he could do now is sit in his car and wait to see what happens. For a full hour he did nothing but listen to music on the radio in hopes it would calm him down but it didn't help in the least. Suddenly there was a tap on the window of his car. He looked over expecting to see a familiar face but what he saw made his heart skip several beats. Gazing through the window was this huge face. It was one of Skinnerbache's henchmen. He now knew what little hope he had of pulling off this job was down the commode.

Suddenly he remembered his gun. He pulled the crazy act before with him and his friend, maybe it will work again. The gun was in the glove compartment and as he reached over to get it the big guy quickly opened the car door and sat down. With a smile ear to ear the big guy said, "Is that where you keep it when you're not acting the tough guy? Todd told me about the whole charade and that you might go for it before you hear me out."

Now Chris was totally confused. He first thought that Todd was forced to tell them their plan and they came down here to take over but, where are the other people? Nothing made sense to him.

Noticing that Chris was deep in thought and somewhere out in space the big guy said, "Hey, hey, earth to Pluto, are you ready to come back to earth?" He chuckled and continued, "It's all right Chris, everything is cool just let me explain. First of all my name is Rolly Farquar. It's a weird name for a black guy but you got to admit it's catchy. I'm not here for the reason you think I am; it's quite the opposite really. I was in the motel alone waiting for Todd while my brother and Skinnerbache went out for something to eat and look for another guy that owes him big bucks; that's another reason we are in Harrisburg. We got to talking and he asked me why my brother and I never went to Las Vegas like we promised. I told him we were waiting around until Skinnerbache got home from the hospital to collect the money he owed us. When he found out we were leaving he blew a gasket and threatened to do something bad to our mother if we left. Of course we love our mom to death and wouldn't want anything to happen to her so we stuck around. We tried to get our mom to go with us to Las Vegas but being she was born, grew up, married, and raised her family in the same neighborhood she refused to go. This left us no choice but to do what we were told. We hated Skinnerbache for what he done to us and now realize the rotten things he was doing to other people that came to him for loans. Many of the people he lent money to were good hard working people that were financially against the wall. Most of them tried borrowing money from banks or loan companies but were turned down simply because they had credit problems. They became desperate and their only recourse was to get the money from Skinnerbache."

Chris interrupted Rolly and asked him what that had to do with the situation at hand and he replied that he and his brother vowed to help Todd out even if all they could do was to prevent anything from happening to his family. "Todd began trusting me and told me what you guys were up to and that you could really use my help. I knew my brother would go along with me on this so I sent him a text message on his cell phone telling him to delay things as long as possible. I'm here to help you pal, what can I do?"

Chris was stunned at what he heard. He couldn't believe that a short while ago this guy Rolly and his brother were out to kick ass and break bones and now they're willing to go the whole nine yards for them.

"I'm curious," said Chris, "How did you and your brother ever get mixed up with Skinnerbache?"

"I don't think we have time for the whole story so here's the short version," replied Rolly, "When we were kids we had diddly squat and we were on the street most of the time trying to hustle some money. We were not bad kids you understand, we didn't rob or cheat. The money we got we earned like running errands, carrying and delivering groceries and the likes. Our mother was, and still is, a God fearing Christian but our father did nothing but drink up all the money the entire family earned. Finally our mother had all she could take and threw him to the curb and we haven't seen him since. We never knew our old man borrowed a thousand dollars from Skinnerbache and one day he appeared at our door demanding the money. There was no way we could pay him so he made me and my brother work for him for two full years to settle the account. I was fifteen and my brother almost seventeen at the time. When our time was up he offered us a job. Without any possible way of getting anything better we accepted. Of course mom doesn't know we are working for him; if she did she would probably die of a heart attack. She thinks we are working for a small loan company collecting bad debts. She's not too thrilled about that job either for she knows how it is to be badgered by collectors. Her only consolation is that we were legitimate; if she only knew."

Chris was a little sadden by Rolly's story and was about to tell him that he and his brother made a wise choice in leaving the scum bag Skinnerbache when suddenly his cell phone rang; it was Spooney calling; "Hey Chris where the hell are you?"

"I'm real close Spooney, just down the street to your right. Is everything all ok?"

"In an excited voice Spooney replied, "Hell yes man, it

couldn't be going any sweeter, cripes man if it keeps going this way I won't need any help from you guys>"

"What's that mean," asked Chris.

"It means man that I'm winning big time. I knocked out three guys since the start of the game and I'm up around ninety thousand dollars. If my luck holds out I could walk out of here without any incident. I want you guys to hold off until you hear from me. Let me try this on my own. Hey, I got to go the break is almost over, I'll talk to you later."

Chris quickly got in the last word before Spooney hung up. "Hey man do you realize that it could take you six to eight hours of playing to do what you want to do? We don't have the luxury of time. Even if you did take first place it would only amount to part of the money, not all of it. You don't know what has gone down with Todd!"

He quickly told him the whole story and Spooney was shocked at the bad news.

Before they hung up Chris said, "Don't be too concerned about Todd and keep your wits about you. We can't afford you being knocked out of the game before we make our play. And the final thing I want you to be aware of is that I won't be coming in alone."

He told him about Rolly and his brother Joshua teaming up with them for a cut of the money. Remembering what they did to him a while back made Spooney a bit nervous.

Checking his watch Chris told Rolly it was a go in thirty minutes.

While they were waiting for the minutes to count down Chris remembered the first encounter with Rolly and Joshua. Their language was terrible and difficult to decipher and now Rolly speaks like an educated person.

Rolly chuckled as he told him they used the hood language just to intimidate and if their dear mother ever heard them speak like that she would have taken a broom to their backs.

Chapter Fifteen

Spooney got back to the table just as the cards were being dealt. He slowly checked the first card and fount the ace of spade. Squeezing the second one every so carefully he found the ace of heart. The odds of having this kind of hand dealt to him are one in two hundred and one. He was on the button meaning only the small and big blind were behind him pre-flop. After that he would know what kind of move everyone made before he decided what he would do. It was a beautiful position to be in as any seasoned poker player would tell you. With pocket aces he was king of the hill. All he had to do was sit back and wait for someone to make a stupid move.

The third and fourth players limped in by calling the big blind but the fifth player came out strong betting $6,000 and everyone behind him folded. When it got to Spooney he quickly raised it to $12,000. Without hesitation the balance of the table mucked their cards, all that is, except the fifth player. He stared at Spooney trying to get some sort of clue as to what his opponent might be holding. Spooney stared back without any emotions whatsoever. For a few moments there was a Mexican standoff until finally Spooney's opponent began counting his chips.

"I got $32,000 chips left and I'm going all in."

Spooney just smiled and pushed in enough chips to cover the all in bet then turned over his pocket aces. He was very surprised to find that his opponent had only a Jack Ten off suit.

Feeling very confident now, Spooney chuckled and said, "Looks as though you under estimated my hand."

His opponent, in his late sixties, was a very gracious man and was known around the circuit as Gentleman Jim. With a smile on his face he replied, "Looks like I made the wrong move at the wrong time. I felt that you had nothing but I see now how wrong I was. Good luck son,"

The dealer pulled all the chips to the center of the table and rapped the table with his knuckles. After the top card was laid aside face down (burned) he took the next three cards from the top of the deck and flopped them over face up.

What Spooney saw laying in front of the dealer were Jack, Jack, seven giving Gentleman Jim a set of Jacks. The percentages shifted from Spooney to Gentleman Jim.

A cold sweat began forming on Spooney's forehead. He was about to lose over 30% of his winning. All he could hope for was an ace on 4th street or the river but it didn't happen. Gentleman Jim raked in the pot doubling his chip stack. He was back in the game and once again a contender.

Would Spooney go "On Tilt"? Being so young it was not hard to do for this was a major blow to his ego.

Meanwhile Chris and Rolly were getting themselves ready to make the big move when suddenly they noticed a local policeman pulling up behind them.

Rolly glanced over to Chris and said very softly, "What the hell are we going to do now man? You got a plan B for this?"

With a concerned look on his face, Chris replied. "I have the foggiest idea what to do man. Here we sit in an out of state automobile, a white guy and a black dude. It doesn't look good at all."

They both sat there very erect staring straight ahead as the policeman exited his car and began walking cautiously toward them.

Chris heard tapping on the side window of his car and slowly turned his head to face a cop with his hand on the handle of his revolver.

"You want to wind down the window sir?"

Chris' mind was reeling. He had no idea what would come out of his mouth when asked why they were parked there. All he could visualize was being cuffed and driven to the station house. He pressed the button and the window lowered automatically.

Both Chris and Rolly continued to stare straight ahead making them more suspicious than they really should be. Rolly began breathing as though he were hyper ventilating which made things worse.

Observing all this, the policeman asked them to put their hands on top of the dash board. "I realize you can park anywhere you wish just as long as it's a legal space to park but some of the locals in the neighborhood told me you've been parked here for an hour or so without leaving your car and that's why they called the station. Now if you have a good enough explanation, one that I can accept, I'll tell the local people there's nothing to worry about and go on with my other duties."

Several moments went by before Chris could bring himself around to speaking for he had no idea what to say. He dare not mention the game that was going on down the street and he knew that all their well laid plans could no longer be carried out. His only priority now was to get out of this precarious situation and keep from being hauled in to the local police station. Todd was at the mercy of Skinnerbache and there was nothing he could do to help him. His only hope was with Rolley's brother Joshua.

He finally told the policeman that they were waiting for a friend that was being dropped off to visit his relatives and then after his visit they were going to take him back home to Baltimore.

"And what is your friend's name?" The policeman asked.

Chris quickly replied that it was Spooney Fenstermacher.

Again Chris was questioned about Spoony's actual first name and he said for the life of him he didn't know and that after all this time the subject of Spoony's actual first name was never brought up. He tried to explain to the officer but it didn't wash.

Of course all of this was an act. He knew that Spooney's real name was Jack Spoon but he didn't want to implicate his friend.

The officer ordered Chris to get out of his car and to lean against the hood. Rolly was told to remain in the car and to keep his hands on top of the dash board.

Without incident Chris did what he was told and as the officer was frisking him he asked if he had anything in the car he should know about. A cold sweat broke out over his entire body as he told him there was a revolver in the glove compartment. With all the excitement he forgot to tell the policeman it was just a plastic gun.

The officer immediately removed his revolver from the holster and ordered Rolly from the car as he radioed for backup. When help arrived both were cuffed and driven to the station house.

Chapter Sixteen

When Todd finished talking with Chris he suddenly heard someone keying the lock and opening the motel door. He didn't have time to explain to Chris that Joshua made sure he could slip through the ropes that were around his wrists. When the door opened Joshua walked in without Skinnerbache. He looked as though there was something terribly wrong. He threw Todd's car keys on the bed and said, "Get to the car Todd while I check out at the front desk, there's not a minute to waste!" He grabbed his belongings and dashed back out the door.

Todd jumped to his feet, not knowing what to expect next, and ran for his car. Several minutes later Joshua came dashing across the parking lot as though he was running the hundred yard dash and jumped in the front seat. Between his rapid breathing he told Todd to get the car moving.

After a few minutes Joshua caught his breath and was able to explain what was going on. He told Todd that he and Skinnerbache found out where the guy lived that owed him money and went to his house. While inside, Skinnerbache threatened him with a whole lot of hurt if he didn't pay up immediately. The guy couldn't come up with the money and

Skinnerbache ordered Joshua to break the fingers on his right hand. The guy ran to his bedroom, got a pistol and shot Skinnerbache through the left eye killing him instantly. He fired a shot at Joshua but somehow missed. Joshua ran out the door, jumped in the car and sped off. The guy had no idea that Joshua had intended to refuse Skinnerbache's order.

While driving south on I-83 Todd placed a call to Chris but there was no answer, just his voice mail asking to leave a message. Assuming they were going through with the heist he left a message to call him immediately.

Meanwhile Chris and Rolly were being questioned by the police. When the authorities found out that Chris' gun was an actor's prop and that they really didn't break any laws, they were obligated to release them, but before leaving the station house they were strongly advised to leave Glen Rock immediately. As they were driving toward the interstate it was quite noticeable that they had a police escort.

As they were traveling on I-83 Chris turned on his cell phone and found that there was a message waiting for him from Todd and immediately returned his call. The news about Skinnerbache was good and bad. The man, although mean and rotten, should not have died that way but on the other side of the coin, it released Todd from his obligation.

Chris was asked to turn around and head north to Todd's house so they could figure out some way to get Spooney and Wendy out of harm's way.

Back in Glen Rock Spooney was recovering from the hand he lost to Gentleman Jim with his pocket aces. He was slowly rebuilding his stack of chips and was almost back to the $90,000 he previously had. He would muck ten to twenty hands until he had decent cards to play with, then he would bet heavily. His cards had to be at least good enough to give him an 80% chance of winning. 'Tight to the vest' was his game plan and it was working well. It was difficult at times to be patient but he knew that was the only way to come out a winner.

He had just mucked his sixth consecutive hand when there was a knock on the door. "This was it!" thought Spooney. He knew he had to act frightened but he was puzzled why they didn't wait for his signal.

Glancing up from the table he caught Wendy's eye. She barely cracked a smile but did manage to give a little wink and looked directly at the door anticipating the arrival of Chris and Todd. Spooney did not bother to tell her about Todd's precarious situation. It would soon be a big payday for her and all her financial problems would be behind her.

Someone from one of the other tables got up, walked to the door and looked through the peep hole. He asked for a name and the voice on the other side identified himself as John Bourne.

Both Wendy and Spooney knew that name and their hearts did a flip-flop. There only hopes were that someone would not tie them in to what happened to him. All they could do was sit back, keep quiet and hope for the best.

The door was opened and Bourne walked in with a scowl on his face. You could readily see he was roaring mad. "Where's the son-of-a-bitch that stranded me?" He walked by every table eye-balling each individual. It was fortunate that Chris was not there.

When asked what happened he told them how he was picked up at the airport by an individual under the pretense of a chauffer and then leaving him at a restaurant somewhere in Maryland.

The tournament director called for a fifteen minute break and asked everyone to stay inside. The door would remain locked and no one would be allowed to enter for the remainder of the tournament.

Just before the fifteen minute break was up he announced that he made a phone call and three of his off duty night watchmen at the lumber company would be outside guarding the house until the game was over. Anyone that chooses to leave would not be permitted to re-enter.

Bourne was still fuming about what had happened to him. It remained a mystery to everyone, everyone except Spooney and Wendy who were figuratively holding their breath in hopes no one would cast suspicion on them.

Suddenly the tournament director realized the break exceeded the fifteen minutes and immediately called everyone back to their tables to resume playing.

Bourne had his $10,000 returned to him and elected to play in the cash game being played by those that were eliminated from the tournament.

As Chris and Rolley pulled into the driveway at Todd's home they noticed that Todd and Joshua were inside waiting for them. Rolley knew that his brother was shot at and was grateful to see his brother safe and sound. After all the greetings the four sat down over a beer to come up with a plan to get Spooney and Wendy out of the precarious position they were put in.

Todd suggested that they phone Spooney and tell him to lose intentionally then get the hell out of there but Chris mentioned that the last time he spoke to him he was up $90,000. He suggested that they let him play out the tournament and maybe, just maybe, he would be lucky enough to win top spot which they estimated at close to $500,000. If he did win maybe Wendy could slide him the bogus bundle of fake money they used to enter and no one would be the wiser.

Joshua disagreed with this idea for it would be a long shot at the very least. He suggested that since no one knew of him or his brother they could pull off the heist without any problems, after all, why should they settle for $500,000 when there is twice that much to be had.

Time was ticking away and one suggestion led to another but none made more sense than Joshua's. With very little time left both Todd and Chris finally agreed to let there new found partners do the job as long as they follow the original plan posing as deputy sheriffs.

Chris went to his car and got the props which consisted of two vests with the lettering 'SHERIFF'S DEPT." on the back which was made by Wendy, and two fake ID's for them to flash when they entered the room. They were instructed to be far enough away from anyone when they showed their ID's so no one could determine they were fakes It was important that they believe the two were real officers of the law without really seeing the ID's close up. Part of not revealing who they really were was to talk and move fast. While performing all these charades Rolley would instruct Wendy to place the money in a bag for evidence while Joshua keeps talking and asking for names. They went over and over what to say and what moves to make to convince everyone they were for real. If it was done right they should be in and out of there in less than seven minutes. Just before leaving with the money Joshua would tell them that there are five more officers outside and they would be coming in to get additional information and to make a final determination if any or all would be spending the night in jail. Todd and Chris would be outside in the car ready to take off the second they exit the door. Finally all four were convinced that this could work. Their only concern was being recognized by the local police that pulled in Chris and Rolley earlier. They discussed this probability on their way to Glen Rock and at the last minute decided there was no solution and that it was a chance they had to take.

They were less than 10 minutes from Glen Rock when Chris'

cell phone rang. It was Spooney calling. "Hey man, what the hell is going on? You guys going to make the hit or are you willing to let me play this thing out? I want you to know that I'm chip healthy; I don't know exactly how healthy but I know it's a lot. One other thing you should know, your buddy John Bourne showed up and he was livid but it's cool though because so far no one has a clue as towhat happened. One other thing, there are now three guys patrolling the outside because of what happened to Bourne. They are employees of the guy that's running this game, night watchmen I think. They shouldn't be hard to handle, just three fat guys that will probably crap themselves when this goes down."

Chris told him they would be there in less than 10 minutes and that two black guys would be replacing them. He reassured him that Rolley and Joshua were working with them and not to worry about what they did to him previously. "Tell Wendy to get the money ready and stuff it in the plastic bag that one of the guys will hand her and to act upset and frightened. Also both of you hang around for as long as it takes to avoid any suspicion then head up to Todd's house. We'll be waiting for you there. Is that clear?"

After he finished talking to Spooney he relayed all the information to Rolley and Joshua. Although there could be some risk they saw no problem in rounding up the three so called guards and taking them inside with them. It should be easy enough to convince them that they are from the sheriff's department.

To avoid getting picked up again by the local authorities Chris and Todd would park the car in an alley down the block and wait seven minutes before returning to pick them up. While waiting, Chris will cover the license plate with a cloth to prevent anyone from writing down the number. When they are far enough away from the scene the cloth will be removed. Their plan was to reroute themselves back to York via various rural routes. Some of these roads are so narrow and dark that only the farm people that live there know they exist and if you weren't careful you could easily end up in some farmers cow pasture. Todd would be the designated driver for he knew this area quite well from his boyhood days.

Chapter Seventeen

They turned the corner and drove mid-way down the block. Chris came to a sudden stop and quickly pointed out the house. Spooney told him earlier that the side entrance is where the game is being held.

With a quick exit from the car, Joshua and Rolley had no problem corralling the three so-called guards. They froze when they saw the sheriff's department vests wanting no part of any confrontation with the law.

Seeing how easy that was, Todd and Chris took off and drove to the back alley. Todd monitored the time while Chris covered the license plate.

Rolley, with his over sized fist, pounded on the door. They waited for a few seconds and pounded again. Finally a voice on the other side said, "Who is it?"

Joshua pushed one of the night watchmen in front of the door so he could be seen through the peep hole. "It's me boss, Charlie; I think you'd better open the door, its two guys from the sheriff's department."

A few seconds went by but the door didn't open. Joshua quickly figured they were trying to hide the money so he motioned his brother to put his shoulder to the door and with one lunge the door flew open.

Joshua was the first one in followed by the three guards with Rolley bringing up the rear. The brothers flashed their bogus ID's and announced that they were deputy sheriffs and then ordered everyone to stay where they were. Rolley caught a movement out of the corner of his eye. It was someone in the back corner kneeling down back of a large wooden desk. "Hey you back of the desk, stand up!"

The man slowly stood up and identified himself as the owner of the house. "You have no cause to bust into my home. This is a private gathering and what you are doing is not legal. My lawyer will be at the Sheriff's office first thing Monday morning. You and your whole damn department will be sued!"

"You do just that mister," Said Joshua, "And while you're at it include the three other deputies that are on there way here to get the necessary information needed to file our reports. Tell your lawyer that all our names will be on those reports for his convenience. I'm sure if he asks nicely someone at the office will make him a copy. Now get over here and stand with the rest of your guests!"

Rolley walked over and looked under the desk. As he suspected the money was there. He pulled a plastic bag from his belt and began looking around the room until he found Wendy. Pointing at her he yelled out, "Hey lady, get over here and put this evidence in the bag and be quick about it!"

Wendy put on her act, being careful not to overdo it, and began bagging the money.

When Spooney first saw Rolley and Joshua enter the room he almost gave it away but quickly realized that if Skinnerbache and his goons were taking over this heist then Todd and Chris could be in serious trouble so he decided to stay in the back of the crowd and keep quiet. If they recognized him it could be lights-out for all three of them and he would be in no position to help his two friends later.

Rolley noticed that Wendy was finished with the money and he immediately dragged it to the door. As he was doing this Joshua instructed everyone to remain in the room and not try to leave. When he got to the door he pretended to speak to one of the phantom deputies that were supposedly standing to the side of the house. This little act certainly convinced everyone that there surely were more deputies waiting outside.

Joshua's last comment to his victims was, "As soon as the deputies secure the outside they will be in to talk to each and everyone. See you in court."

Todd and Chris had it timed perfectly. They pulled up with the trunk already opened and waited for the two brothers to throw the money in and then sped down the street toward their back road route.

Several minutes passed without the appearance of the three deputies that were supposedly outside. It was nearly ten minutes until several of the players wised up and realized this was a hit and run heist. John Bourne was the first to suspect this and walked outside to find no one there. Now realizing that he was delayed purposely by one of the people that just walked off with his share, he became irate. Out of his mouth came some of the most foul and unholy words that were ever spoken by man.

Several of the players began talking. "Why would he make such a scene in front of everyone? Was this an act to throw off any suspicion that he may have been part of what just went down?" Some of the players, including his friend from Scranton, had reason to think so. It stood to reason now that he might have made up the story about being stranded by some unknown driver. He lost his money but maybe only for a short while.

Spooney walked across the room and sat next to Wendy. He whispered, "Do you realize the two guys that left with the money are the same guys that sent me to the hospital? They work for Skinnerbache. I don't feel good about all this. You know what I think? I think Skinnerbache and his goons forced our scheme out of Todd and then took over. All of this planning and risk taking was for nothing. Were screwed Wendy! Let's give it another ten minutes and get the hell out of here."

Wendy nervously replied, "I hope you're wrong Spooney, I agree that the sooner we exit this place the better. If these guys start putting two and two together they are going to suspect you also, being that you were first on the waiting list and I'll have to explain how you, as an unknown, got there in the first place."

While everyone was still in a state of confusion, Spooney slowly walked to the door leading into the living room and quickly left by the front door. Wendy acted as though she was going to faint and asked her boss if she could go home. He saw no reason for her to stay and gave her permission to leave.

Without any incident Todd got everyone back to his house in less than 45 minutes which was at least 20 minutes longer than traveling the interstate but for safety sake it was worth the extra time. He parked the car in the garage and closed the door before opening the trunk lid. Joshua and Rolley grabbed the sides of the bag and carried it through the kitchen to the living room and dumped the bundles of money on the carpet. There was exactly $990,400 laying there for all to admire. The four reveled in their success and congratulated each other with high fives and hand shakes. Todd broke out the booze to further celebrate while waiting for Spooney and Wendy to show up.

Todd stood up and lifted his glass to toast their success. "I should wait until the other two get here before I make this announcement but I'm bursting at the seams. If it had not been for Rolley and Joshua we would not be here gazing upon nearly $1,000,000. All they asked for was $50,000 each so they could start a new life and take care of their beloved mother, and that they shall receive, but while we waited for these two guys to do the hard part of the job Chris and I decided that since I was no longer obligated to pay the $65,000 to Skinnerbache it should go to these two guys for doing a great job and to Wendy we are going to add another $35,000 to her purse. Why are we doing this? Well, we don't like odd dollar amounts."

The two brothers were shocked and grateful at what they heard. They now had $165,000 between them and immediately began discussing just how they would convince their mother to leave the neighborhood she cherished and move to Las Vegas with them.

Soon after Wendy and Spooney pulled into the driveway and noticed the lights were on but the shades pulled down. Still concerned that his friends were in trouble he kept the motor running in preparation of getting the hell out of there. Using his cell phone he dialed Todd's home phone number. It rang just one time and he heard "Hello" at the other end, it was Chris's voice.

It took some time to convince Spooney that everything was on the up and up before he and Wendy came it. Actually Todd had to come outside to prove to him it was all right. Then, and only then, did he believe the story Chris told him on the phone.

Wendy was ecstatic about the bonus she was receiving. Finally she would be debt free and able to live a normal life. She was advised to work for her boss at least one more month before quitting her job.

The celebration went on into the early morning hours before the brothers and Wendy left for home.

Todd waited until 9 a.m. then phoned his wife to tell her that everything was all right and to come home immediately. He explained to her that his big time gambling days were over and apologized for all the stress and anxiety he caused her and the children. Being the loving wife and mother that she was, she agreed to return home that same day.

After he hung up the phone he told his friends the good news and the three went out to the local restaurant for breakfast.

Wouldn't one think that after all the money they now had in their possession there would be no concern about the four $100 bills that were used to cover the bogus $10,000 entry fee? As they were eating a hearty breakfast all they could talk and argue about was whose bills were whose.

For several weeks after the heist they checked the newspaper and TV for any news about what had happened but there was none. It was probably left unreported due to the many different people at the game such as several lawyers, one judge, one leader of a very well known church and many prominent people that were pillars of their community. One does have to wonder what ever happened to Mr. John Bourne.

Todd's family was back to normal and with out fear of any reprisals.

Chris and Spooney moved to the York area and became partners with Todd in a distributorship of advertising products which developed into a very successful business.

Approximately six months later they received a phone call from Joshua and Rolley. They finally got to Las Vegas after a long period of convincing their mother to take up roots and go with them. After attending dealer school they both landed jobs in one of the largest casinos in town.

Before the three guys knew it a year went by without a card being dealt or a bet being made, that is until one Friday afternoon when the week was winding down Spooney brought up the subject of the four $100 bills used in the heist. To finally put this issue to rest the three sat at the conference table and played no limit Texas hold-em for the money. It really doesn't matter who won the $400, what really mattered was that they enjoyed the competition tremendously.

Where did this innocent little game go from there? Was it a game soon forgotten or was it like an alcoholic testing his will after years of sobriety?

Chapter Eighteen

The start of their second year of business was so successful they decided to take on a few employees to help with the work load. Two salesmen and a billing clerk were added to their staff, freeing the three of them up to do the much needed administrative work and decision making, something that previously they had to squeeze in between sales calls and order writing.

Todd had a full days work behind him but decided to stay a few more hours to go over a huge order before sending it to the manufacturer. When he was sure everything was in order he placed it into an envelope and put it on his secretary's desk to be mailed out the following morning.

He went back to his office to relax for a few moments before heading for home. He no sooner sat down in his chair when the phone rang. It was his wife calling to find out when he was coming home. He looked up at the clock on the wall and was surprised to see that it was 9 p.m. She told him the kids were fed and getting ready for bed and asked him if she should continue keeping his dinner warm for him. He told her not to bother that he would be home soon and eat left-overs.

After hanging up the phone he decided to turn on the office TV to check out the weather. As he was going from one channel to the other he noticed that The World Series of Poker was airing and unconsciously stopped flipping channels. Sitting at the table were some of the world's most recognized players.

He was startled when the phone rang. It seemed only a few minutes ago that Deb had phoned him but she reminded him that it was over an hour ago.

From his office to home was nearly a fifteen minute drive. While driving he began to fantasize that he was a finalist at the WSOP with all those great players that he saw on TV. With a huge stack of chips he was sitting next to Doyle "Dolly" Brunson and on the other side of him was the Unabomber. He was just about to call a large bet made by Brunson when the loud sound of an air horn brought him back to reality. He was merging onto the highway and nearly sideswiped a tractor trailer. He kept this near accident to himself realizing just how stupid it was.

A week went by without any thought of poker until one Friday afternoon when business was winding down he got on his office computer and down loaded one of the better poker sites. He didn't think there was anything wrong if he opened a small checking account at a bank other that the one his business or family dealt with. He would only deposit a few hundred dollars to cover his electronic fund transfers. He chalked it up as merely entertainment money, nothing more. No one had to know, after all, he needed some relaxation and it wouldn't hurt anyone.

It took about a week for the funds to transfer to the poker site. When he was notified that the funds were in his account he began playing immediately. To test the waters he started small, $5.00 plus $1.00 and soon found out that it was very different from the way he used to play. He soon learned that for a mere $6.00 the players would call or go "all-in" on anything. After a month of playing he finally gave it up as a bad experience and closed out his account at the poker website and the bank. This was not for him for he now realized that the only way to play solid poker was at a table of live people, ones you could analyze, and ones that knew how to play the game properly.

Over the next several months he had the desire to play Texas Hold-em but not the obsession he once had, one that nearly drove him into bankruptcy, a divorce, maybe even costing his life. This he swore would never happen again and he sincerely meant it.

Spring finally arrived and it was welcomed after a long and hard winter. Todd and his partners had their golf clubs out and polished for the upcoming first outing since late last fall. Last summer they took several lessons from the local pro. Their handicaps were quite high but this did not bother them all that much. All they wanted to accomplish at this point in time was to hone their skills, have fun and get some exercise.

The following Tuesday developed into a perfect day for golfing so the three took the afternoon off and headed for the links. As they were about to tee off Todd's cell phone rang. It was his secretary telling him there was a call from some guy named Joshua in Las Vegas and he wanted his call returned as quickly as possible. She said the call sounded quite urgent.

As soon as Todd hung up he immediately dialed Joshua's number. The phone didn't finish its second ring when he heard his friend's voice. "What's up buddy? My secretary said your call seemed urgent. Is everything alright?"

"Not exactly Todd, as a matter of fact things are rotten in Vegas. Rolley got bamboozled by a couple of local sharks. They cheated him out of all the money you gave him."

"How in hell did that happen?" Todd asked.

Joshua went on to tell him that the two sharks talked him into a three handed no limit cash game of Texas hold-em. The one guy was a fancy dealer (one who can stack the cards) and every third hand he would set up his brother with a straight and at the same time deals his buddy a flush. The next time he got the deal he might give my brother two big pair then deal his cohort a set (three of a kind). While he was setting Rolley up he would fold and let the two play out the hand. When the other guy was dealing the cards they would both fold and let my brother have the blinds (forced bets). When Rolley dealt they would only play if they definitely felt they could win. Every third hand was very expensive for my brother and in about four hours he was cleaned out. This was a nest egg he wanted to hang on to for the future but now it's gone. I found about these two guys from a friend that knew all about them. I really feel bad for him; do you have any ideas how we could get his money back? I would appreciate any help or advice you could send my way."

Todd told him to sit tight and wait for a call from him on Wednesday.

After nine holes the three went to the club house for refreshments and some serious discussion regarding Joshua's phone call. They felt committed to help since the two brothers stepped in and helped them in their hour of need. Without them they would definitely not be where they are today.

It was agreed that the three would fly to Vegas with a plan. What that plan would be was yet to be worked out. Spooney suggested they bring a fourth guy with them. It was a friend of his that lived in his home town of Westminster, Maryland by the name of Texas Eddie. He moved east to be closer to Atlantic City which he preferred over Las Vegas and is a magician with a deck of cards. Texas Eddie was known around the gambling scene as 'The Instrument'. He could deal you anything you asked for and without being detected by the best of them. He was recently banned by the Atlantic City casinos for counting cards in black jack. "I have his phone number; do you want me to call him to set up a meeting for this evening?"

It was quite evident that they would need someone of this expertise to pull off a scam of this nature, especially against two that already knew the game of deceit.

Spooney made the call and the meeting was set for eight p.m. that evening at the office.

Texas Eddie was well received by everyone. He had an air of confidence which is one of the prime requisites for this type of operation. The last thing you want is someone dealing the cards with shaky hands and a sweaty brow. You could tell this man had been around the block several times.

After hearing their story from beginning to end he chuckled and shook his head in disbelief. "You guys are the luckiest sons-of-bitches on God's green earth, you know that don't you? You're up against professionals this time and they would pick-up on your little scam five minutes into the game. I have a plan to get your friends money back but you will have to trust me and follow my instructions to the letter. I want you to understand that I don't do this type of thing for nothing but that doesn't mean any monies should come out of your pockets. It is my understanding that your friend is out $65,000 and my fee for something like this is $10,000 plus expenses. If things go right everyone must agree that we sit at the table until we win $76,000. My expenses shouldn't be more than $1,000. If everyone agrees to this we will go over my plan and head for Vegas."

This was more than the three guys had hoped for, especially if the two con men will be paying Texas Eddie's fee. Spooney got up from his chair and shook his hand saying, "It's a deal man, let's hear your plan."

Texas Eddie smiled and replied, "You know, all this talking

and scheming makes a person thirsty as hell and the thirst I have will not be quenched with water or soda, if you catch my meaning."

Chris went to his office and returned with a bottle of bourbon and four glasses. After a few shooters Texas Eddie was ready to divulge his plan.

For him to deal the right cards to the right people there could only be five players. Until the deal gets to Texas Eddie they were told to play very conservative when either Chris or Todd deals, bet only if they are very sure they had the winning hand. When either of the two con men deal make occasional bets then fold. Since Texas Eddie has twice the amount of money as the other two he will do most of the losing to them so as not to queer the set up. When the deal gets to Texas Eddie they should expect power hands. When they get these power hands they were told to slow-play most of them and let their two adversaries try to push them out. If they fold Texas Eddie would use the one, two, three chip signal by capping his cards with chips. If there is one chip that will mean he is to win and the other two will muck their cards, if two chips are shown that will mean Chris is to take the pot, if three chips then Todd is to win while the other two muck without showing their cards and if no chips are capping his cards then both Todd and Chris should fold pre-flop and let Texas Eddie play out the hand with the option to win or lose depending on his good judgment. If this is played to perfection their scam would go undetected. Spooney would be the security guy in case something went wrong. Once they land in Vegas each one would go their separate way as complete strangers with reservations at four different hotels. Todd will check the brothers to find out how he could contact the two con men. When he gets this information he will phone Texas Eddie to set up the game. Chris was chosen as one of the players because of his previous acting experience. He would show Todd how to dress and act likes a super nice guy from the mid-west with a lot of money but no experience in playing Texas hold-em. It would be necessary to bring at least $40,000 in cash with them, $20,000 for Texas Eddie and $10,000 each for Todd and Chris. Texas Eddie, over a period of two hours will purposely loose more than the other two in order to make it appear like he is a bad player. Chris will win most of the money and Todd only several thousand. This could not be done quickly for they might suspect something. It would probably take four or five hours. When the $76,000 plus the initial $40,000 is in their hands the game will end. Chris will pretend to be anxious to play more but Texas Eddie and Todd will decline because they would have to head back home to get ready for the next work week. He would then ask the two con men if they would like to play a three handed game the following day at noon. This should give them an opportunity they would jump at and will very likely agree to. It would satisfy them knowing that they would get their money back the following day plus all of Chris' cash. Todd will make arrangements to meet with the brothers and return all of Rolley's money. The following morning the four of them would high-tail it back home satisfied with a job well done.

The following day Todd phoned Joshua to tell him they would be on a plane for Vegas Friday afternoon.

Chapter Nineteen

It was early afternoon when their plane touched down in the great city often referred to as the metropolis of great expectations. Many people come here hoping to leave millionaires but find they hardly have enough money for air fare home. As P. T. Barnum once said, "there's a sucker born everyday" and that is what the casinos bank their money on. There is no record of a gambling establishment going belly-up due to customers continuously breaking the bank.

They each took a separate cab and headed for their respective hotels. As soon as Todd checked in and got to his room he phoned Joshua. When his friend heard Todd's voice he was elated, "Hey Todd where are you?"

"I'm in a hotel downtown big guy," replied Todd, "We just got in less than an hour ago and we brought another person with us, an expert in dealing Texas hold-em, you might say. If everything goes right, and I have no doubt that it will, we'll have Rolley's money back in his pocket very soon. I'll spare you all the details for the moment, but now I need to know how we can come in contact with the two guys that took your brother's money."

Joshua told him they went by the names of Bart Bigelow, aka

Bart the Fart, a huge white guy with premature white hair. "He is in his thirties and weighed about 250 pounds, sports a large beer belly and carries a scar above his left eyebrow. He almost always dresses like in the 1970's, wearing leisure suits." He cautioned Todd not to call him Bart the Fart for he takes offense to it. "The other guy would be in his thirties also, a small black guy by the name of Nemo that has often been mistaken for Sammy Davis, Jr. Their primary hang out is in what the locals refer to as the loser's lounge but is really called the Royale club. Invariably they would find some poor sucker looking for a last chance to get some of his money back." He went on to say that this lounge had always been the central point for people looking to play in a private game figuring they had a better chance than at the casino.

The information was immediately passed on to Texas Eddie. He told Todd to phone Chris and both show up at the loser's club in two hours. They were instructed to come separately and sit at different ends of the bar with no communication between them.

Texas Eddie got to the lounge fifteen minutes earlier so he could identify Bigelow and Nemo. He sat at the middle of the bar and scanned the entire room but saw no one fitting their description. An hour and forty-five minutes passed and in walked Chris. A few minutes later Todd entered the room. Sitting at either end of the bar they eye-balled Texas Eddie. Catching their stare he slowly shook his head left and right indicating Bigelow and Nemo were not there. Several hours went by and when they were about to call it a night the two walked in and sat at a table across the room. Both Todd and Chris became a little nervous but Texas Eddie sat there as cool as a cucumber.

After several minutes passed, Texas Eddie got up from his bar stool and walked over to the quarter slot machine located next to where Bigelow and Nemo were sitting. He reached in his pocket, pulled out several quarters, and began feeding the one arm bandit.

He dumped all his quarters without success then pulled out a roll of bills. The roll of bills was so big he could hardly extract it from his pocket. This caught the immediate attention of Bigelow and Nemo. Texas Eddie looked over his shoulder at the bar then made the comment, "Damn, I'm out of quarters! I feel this bandit it about to pay off and if I leave I know someone will jump in and win my money. Any of you gentlemen have any quarters you'd care to exchange for bills"?

He held the roll close enough for them to see that he was carrying a huge amount of large bills, $50's and $100's.

Nemo was the first to speak out, "No man, we don't carry that much change in our pockets. You sure you want to continue playing this machine? It'll string you out until it gets all your money, believe me, it's not a good way to gamble. You like playing poker?"

With a smile, Texas Eddie replied, "Yeah, I play some. Back home in Iowa I play once a month with my friends and I must say I'm not all that bad, or should I say I get lucky every once in a while. You guys play?"

Bigelow chimed in, "We're like you, we play every once in a while, nothing to speak of. I got lucky earlier at the casino playing in a Texas hold-em cash game. It's the first time I won anything. Like you, I got lucky."

Texas Eddie offered his hand and shook Bigelow's hand, "Well, good for you! It's not often guys like us come out a winner; It's usually the seasoned player that wins. My name is Bertram but my friends call me Bart."

The two introduced themselves and asked Texas Eddie to sit down and have a drink with them.

Meanwhile at the bar Chris and Todd wondered what the conversation was between the three at the table but they were confident that Texas Eddie was reeling them in. Bigelow and

Nemo were unaware it was a reverse sting and never realized that this time they had the proverbial hook in their mouths.

After a few drinks with his victims, Texas Eddie got up from the table and walked to the bar. Besides Todd and Chris there were five other people at the bar, three women and two men. Before approaching them he said something to the other five. The three women seemed amused at what he said and the two men, more or less, told him to move on or get lost, something to that effect. He then went to where Todd was sitting and whispered, "The game is on in one hour. Stay sitting and I'll get back to you." He then approached Chris with the same message and returned to Bigelow and Nemo's table.

"There are two guys at the bar that seem interested in playing. Do you want me to ask them over so we can introduce ourselves?"

Bigelow raised his arm and signaled Todd and Chris over.

Todd introduced himself as Earl from Arkansas and Chris used the name of Clyde from West Virginia.

Nemo was the next to speak, "I understand you two gentlemen would like to play some Texas hold-em. We like a friendly game, $10 and $20 blinds, no limit with a $2,500 buy in. Are you interested?"

Chris spoke up saying, "Wow! That's pretty steep; I'm not used to playing for that much money, do I have time to go to the ATM? My wife would kill me if she knew I was playing in a game like this."

Bigelow assured him there was plenty of time.

Texas Eddie suggested they use his hotel room for the game but, being cautious, Begelow suggested they play at a neutral spot by renting a motel outside of Vegas. He knew of one where they would not be disturbed.

This is not what Texas Eddie expected but he agreed to his

suggestion nevertheless. He knew Spooney would be close by in case they needed him.

Nemo gave them the address and told them to meet there in one hour.

The trio was pleased to have this extra time to review their game plan and to pass all this information on to Spooney.

By now they felt relatively safe to be together so they decided to go back to the bar for a drink and contact Spooney.

As they sipped their cocktails Chris asked Texas Eddie what he said to the other people sitting at the bar that made the women smile and the men frown. He replied, "Well, I asked the women if they would like to come to my room to see my paintings, and I asked the men for a few dollars to hold me over until I got home. They didn't believe me when I promised to mail them a check."

Todd tapped him on the shoulder and smiled, "You old dog, you're sure good at what you do."

With fifteen minutes to go before game time they hailed a cab and were on their way.

As the cab pulled up in front of the motel they noticed Spooney inside, he was apparently registering for a room. They hoped he could get a room next to theirs, or at least close by. Todd looked over at Chris and commented, "Hope you didn't forget the fake pistol to give our fearless guard.

With a concerned look on his face, Chris replied, "Let's hope to God it's not necessary for him to use it."

Todd chuckled and replied, "Knowing Spooney I'm sure he'll worked wonders with that piece of plastic, just like you did when Skinnerbache had us against the wall. You made him act out the scene many times before we left for Vegas so relax."

Spooney noticed them exiting the cab and caught their eye with a wink and a smile. As he turned around to give his credit card to the attendant at the desk he placed his left hand in back of him and signaled thumbs up indicating he would be close by and waiting for a phone call if anything went awry. He was on everyone's speed dial and one ring would bring him running.

After several knocks on the door it, was answered by Nemo and he laughingly commented, "Welcome gentlemen, hope you didn't pray too hard to the poker gods. Before we get started, would anyone like a drink? We got beer. Bourbon and a variety of soft drinks for those that want to stay sober."

They passed on drinks and sat down ready to play some poker. Texas Eddie quickly noticed that Nemo scrambled to get the chair immediately to the left of his partner. He knew that very likely meant they were going to exercise the card switching game. With a lot of practice between the two they can pull a card from the bottom of their two down cards, lay it on their leg and switch cards if it would help their partner's hand. There are subtle signals they can give to each other indicating what they need and if the other one has it then a switch is made. As long as he knew what was going down it would not be necessary to alert Todd or Chris, if they knew it could queer the whole set-up. He saw this type of scam before and knew how to handle the situation when he was dealing.

The cards were spread out on the table and each one picked a card. Texas Eddie was fortunate enough to pull an ace which meant he was the first one to deal.   Chris   was   sitting immediately to Texas Eddie's left, followed by Todd, Bart and Nemo.

The two cards were dealt to each player. Chris was pleased to see that he had pocket tens. Todd checked his cards to find big slick suited (Ace and King of hearts). Both were anxious to dump some chips in the center of the table but noticed Texas Eddie had one chip capping his cards. This meant that both Chris and Todd were to fold even though they both had their blind chips invested.

Todd glanced over at Texas Eddie in hopes he would change the chip to three and let him play this hand but he got no response from him, just a blank stare. Bart raised Todd's $20 blind to $100 leaving it up to Nemo to fold, call or raise the bet. He looked at his two cards several times giving Bart time to signal him to pass a particular card if he had one that he needed. Sure enough, Nemo's hand went to his lap almost at the same time Bart's hand dropped. It was evident to Texas Eddie that they were switching cards. They did a pretty good job of it for if he was not up to their game it would have gone unnoticed by anyone at the table. Nemo folded but Texas Eddie called the $100 to go. Reluctantly Chris and Todd mucked their hands. The flop came up Ace (spade), king (diamond) and 4 (heart). The flop did nothing for Chris but it would have given Todd two pair. He strongly felt that he could have won the hand but this was not what their expert dealer wanted. He had to have faith in him for he was the man with the magic fingers and the plan.

With only two remaining in the game Bart pushed in $500 and Texas Eddie called. Fourth street was dealt and a 6 (heart) was shown. Bart checked and Texas Eddie checked with him. The river was dealt and another ace (club) was turned over. Without hesitation Bart bet another $500 and was quickly called. Bart flipped over his cards showing two sixes and said, "All I got is a full house, three sixes and a pair of aces."

"You got a winner," replied Texas Eddie

Todd nearly fell out of his chair. He wanted to tell their man that would have been his chips plus a lot more if only he would have allowed him to play. He once again tried to catch his attention but was not able to make eye contact.

Things didn't go well for the three men the first hour of play. Although Chris and Todd were not out all that much, their partner was, and to the tune of $2,500, forcing him to buy another

125

$2,500 worth of chips. They had to believe what their leader said at the outset that he would guarantee they would get Rolley's money back for him.

Another hour passed and it was the same as the first one only Texas Eddie was now out over $7,000. Noticing the concern on their faces, he suggested they take a ten minute break for some refreshments which everyone agreed to. "My knee keeps slipping out of its socket," he said, "I need to work it back in place, Earl, (Todd's fictitious name), could you give me a hand and hold my ankle?"

Texas Eddie really has had this problem with his knee for a long time but he only used this as an excuse to be able to talk to Todd while the other three were pouring themselves a drink. He sat in the chair and partially stretched out his left leg while Todd bent over and held his ankle. In a whisper, he told Todd not to be so concerned about the way the game was going and to have faith in him. "I got them right where I want them and in another hour we'll have our money, trust me, and now get your damn hands off my leg before I start thinking your gay!"

Todd chuckled, "You're the boss, lets go get 'em."

It was Nemo's deal when they resumed playing. Texas Eddie had the small blind and Todd the big blind. When the two cards were dealt to everyone Texas Eddie glanced out of the corner of his eye to see if any cards were switched and to his surprise found that they weren't. Apparently both were satisfied with what they were dealt or they were holding cards that could not help the other one. Todd, being the first one to act, glanced to his right to find their leader had no chips capping his cars. He cupped his hands around his cards and checked the first card; it was a three (heart). He slid that card to the top and checked the second one; it was a three (spade). To say the least, this was, in no way a hand he should get involved in but it was the best hand he saw since he had big slick so he decided to speculate and limped in with $20.

It was now Bart's turn to act. He fumbled around for a minute then called the $20 and Nemo promptly folded as well as Texas Eddie and Chris. The flop came up ace, three, 5, all different suits. This gave Todd a set of threes but little did he know that Bart was holding a 2 and 4 giving him the baby straight. He checked to Bart hoping he had a pair of aces and would come out with a sizeable bet. He discounted the possibility of a straight which meant Bart would have had to call the big blind with a 2 and 4 and he gave him more credit than to do that, but he was dead wrong. Nemo might also have some dealing skills but it would be pretty obvious to Texas Eddie if he did and he hadn't noticed any in the first hour.

Bart hesitated for a while then came out with a hefty $750 bet. Now, Todd's thinking took a different turn. His thoughts now were leaning toward the possibility of him holding a pocket pair of aces or fives which would give him a bigger set. He shuffled his cards four of five times then started stacking and re-stacking his chips. Several minutes went by and finally Bart asked him to make a decision one way or another. Indicating confidence he sat back in his chair and crossed his arms across his chest.

Todd played enough poker to know that when someone acts this way it means one of two things, it's an act to make you believe they have a hand, which is something a seasoned player would do, or, they don't realize what they are doing and most certainly have a power hand. He had to make a decision whether it was worth another $750 to see fourth street and much more to find out what the river might bring. He weighed the odds of the possibility of catching a pair on the board for a full house and found that he had nine possible outs. Reluctantly he counted out $750 in chips and placed them neatly in the center of the table.

Nemo took the top card of the deck and laid it aside. Fourth street was flipped over and Todd could not believe what he saw; it was the fourth three. He quickly checked his hand which normally indicates that particular card did nothing to help. The trap was set and he waited for his opponent to act on his hand. It was now time for Bart to put on his little act. He checked his hole cards several times, looked up at the ceiling then over at Todd. Finally he counted out another $750 in chips and threw them to the center of the table.

Now it was Todd's turn to put on an act; he picked up his cards and held them between his fingers as though he was going to fold and then laid them back down and sighed. "Part of me says fold and another part tells me to call, I don't know what to do."

Once again Bart sits back in his chair and folds his arms. Staring straight at Todd he commented, "Two pair ain't gonna cut it my man, at least I don't think so." He put his hand to his unshaven face and scratched the end of his nose.

Todd glanced around the room in an effort to catch a glimpse of Chris and Jonsey. They were staring right at him with the look on their face that appeared to be saying, "Lay it down, he's got you beat, don't call the bet!" Little did they know he had the rock solid nuts.

Nemo sat there quietly and without any expression. He was quite sure his partner had the sucker beat and hoped his partner didn't scare the guy off with his sizeable bet and big mouth.

Bart was now very confident he had this mid-western bumpkin Earl (Todd) right where he wanted him. His only concern was that maybe he should have bet more money to prevent him from sucking out on the river card.

Todd stared at Bart for a solid minute without saying a word. Bart returned the stare with a smirk on his face. Finally Todd spoke, "Well, my friend, you were half right when you called my hand; I only got one pair but I don't think you have anything so

I'm going to invest another $750 to prove to myself that I read you right." He counted out the chips then sat back and waited for Nemo to deal the river card, a card that didn't mean anything to him.

Nemo dealt the river card showing a red king. Looking directly into the bloodshot eyes of Bart, he wasn't quite sure if it was a heart or diamond, but it didn't matter in the least for he knew he had the man roped and hog tied. Trying not to look as confident as he felt, he said, "Check to the man with the power hand."

Bart checked his hole cards one more time then looked up at Todd and smiled. In an effort to appear weak, Todd put his head between his hands and looked down at the table.

This gesture confirmed Bart's belief that Todd had, at the best, two pair and firmly believed the bumpkin would call another $750 so he splashed it on the table and smiled. "One never knows, two pair just might take the pot, and a healthy pot it is."

Now it was Todd's turn to create some doubt. "You know what? You're sure making it tough on yourself. I am very sure my two pair is the best hand so I will raise your bet to $1,500.

It was now up to Bart to re-raise, call or fold. He asked himself; "Was his little straight good enough to take down this yokel or was this bumkin stupid enough to go over the top with only two pair?"

He looked across the table at Todd and became more confused than ever when his adversary smiled then began to chuckle. Todd was putting on the best performance of his life appearing inexperienced at the game of bluffing.

Finally Bart made the decision to call the raise and as he splashed another $750 in the center of the table, he said, "I think that's all you have is two pair and I should make you pay another $750 to see my straight." He threw up his cards showing a five high straight, and then said, "Let's see your two pair."

Todd continued to smile and flipped over his pair of threes, I didn't lie to you, I got a pair of red threes and a pair of black ones. That's what they call it back home but I guess here in Vegas you would call it quads."

Bart's jaw nearly dropped to his knees when he saw Todd's hand. His stomach did a flip-flop and his blood pressure must have risen 50 points but he was able to maintain his cool and commented, "Good hand," nothing more than those two words, "Good hand."

"Thanks," replied Todd. "And thank you Nemo for dealing me such a great hand."

Nemo said nothing in return, he merely gathered the cards together and handed them over to Eddie but he could feel his partner's laser like glare on the back of his head.

The rest of the evening went precisely as was planned it. For the following hour he allowed Bart and Nemo to win some of their money back just to avoid any suspicion. From then on when he was dealing he would lose first to Todd and then to Chris but only once to either Bart or Nemo making it two to one in favor of the home team Another time he would deal a power hand to Chris and a strong hand to either or both Bart and Nemo. Their hands were good enough to call but never good enough to win. Sometimes Todd would stay in the hand and other times fold making it look legitimate.

It was a long and drawn out game but it had to be done that way to make it appear up and up. Texas Eddie could have taken them for all they had in less than two hours but that was not the way the game is played safely. The last thing any of them wanted was to get hurt in the process even though Spooney was close by to back them up.

By 2:30 a.m. Chris quickly calculated that they had the $76,000 won between them with him being the big winner. He looked over at Eddie and nodded indicating they had the money they were after. At the same time he nudged Todd's leg with his foot indicating they had enough. Todd was the first to speak up, "Well gentlemen, I'm calling it a night. I have a plane to catch very early this morning; would someone want to cash me in?"

Texas Eddie spoke up, "Couldn't you play for a few more hours? I'm out a lot of money."

Todd declined and began putting on his jacket. "It's going to be a long flight and I've only got a few hours to sleep. If I wasn't going back tomorrow morning I would stay but I'm a working stiff and need to show up for work first thing Monday."

Texas Eddie rose from his chair and stretched, "Guess I'll have to lick my wounds and get some rest also."

Bart and Nemo were quite aware that Chris was the big winner and they were not about to let him walk out the door with their money. Bart was the first one to speak. He looked across the table at Chris and said, "Hey man, you want to play some three handed poker?"

Chris looked up from counting his money and said with a smile, "Yeah man, I'd love to! How about giving me a couple hours to get something to eat and freshen up then meet me at my hotel; we can play there. I'll give you guys a chance to get some of your money back."

Nemo asked what hotel he was staying out and Chris pulled his key card from his wallet and showed it to them. "Meet me there between 5:30 and 6:00 and I'll be ready to play some more."

Bart asked, "How do we know you'll be there?"

Showing no fear and utilizing some of his acting experience, he rose from his chair and pointed his finger directly at both of them, "Sir, I'm from PawPaw, West Virginia and when we give you our word you can take it to the bank. If you have enough money to buy in at $5,000 then be there and ready to play."

"What are you trying to do man," complained Nemo, "This game was only a $2,500 buy in, so why are you doubling the stakes?"

"It's simple," replied Chris, "You're trying to win your money back and I'm giving you that chance but you have to take some risk to win it back. You got to agree that's fair."

Texas Eddie and Todd were holding their breath for they hadn't expected anything like this to happen. Todd had his cell phone out and ready to speed dial Spooney if this went much further.

Bart motioned Nemo to the other side of the room. They spoke so low that no one was able to hear what they were saying. Finally Bart walked to the table and said, "Okay man, we'll be there at 5:30 sharp; be sure you have a couple decks of cards."

With a sigh of relief Texas Eddie quickly called for a taxi and the three left the room. While waiting for the cab they stood in front of the office where there was plenty of light. At the same time Todd called Spooney and told him what went down. He didn't realize that he was right in back of them sitting in front of a slot machine in the lobby of the motel.

It was not long until the cab arrived and they headed back to their respective hotels. While in transit, Spooney noticed a car following them. He pointed this out to the other two and they all agreed that it was Bart and Nemo behind them. They were most likely following to make sure Chris was not going to skip out on his deal.

Chris was the first one to be dropped off at his hotel. Before he got out of the cab he made sure he knew where Todd was staying and then told him to expect him to show up in approximately 15 minutes for he would need a place to stay. He planned to walk into his hotel and tell the man at the desk he was checking out. Since he used his credit card there was no reason for him to come back to sign anything. All he had to do was get his things and leave unnoticed.

After checking in at the front desk he immediately took the elevator to the third floor and got his bags which were already packed and ready to go. He then hurried to the back of the building and took the stairs back down to the lobby and exited the back of the building to the street opposite the side of the hotel where he hailed a cab.

Texas Eddie went with Todd to his hotel and Spooney followed shortly thereafter. As they were sipping a drink they heard a knock on the door, it was Chris. The sting was all but completed. All they had left to do was count their winnings, phone Joshua and Rolley to pick up their money, pay off their man with the magic fingers and get the hell out of Vegas.

The call was made, "Hello Josh, this is your friend Todd. Guess what? We got your brother's money." In the background you could hear Josh waking his brother telling him the good news. "We hope you can come by right away to pick it up. Bart and Nemo are tailing Chris and we need to find somewhere to stay other than downtown Vegas until our flight leaves this morning."

Joshua replied, "Let me know where you are and we will swing by and pick you guys up, hell man, you can stay at our place until it's time to leave. Our mom has always wanted to meet you anyway and she'll cook us a big breakfast."

In less than thirty minutes Todd's phone rang; it was Joshua calling from the rear of their hotel waiting for them.

After a scrumptious breakfast of eggs, bacon and home fries the men went to the living room to settle up with the money. Todd opened a large plastic shopping bag and dumped the bills on the coffee table. "Rolley, I'm sorry we couldn't get all your money back but I think you'll be happy with what we have for you. We knew we were close to what you lost but were unable to calculate to the dollar what we had in front of us. We invested $40,000 which we deducted and Texas Eddie's fee for setting this whole thing up is $10,000 plus $1,000 for expenses which leaves a balance of $63,600. I'm sorry to say big guy, you're out $1,400. I realize our card dealer didn't come cheap but believe me; he earned every cent of it. Without him this could have never happened so I think he deserves a round of applause and, incidentally, don't ever play poker with this man."

Rolley walked up to Todd and gave him a bear hug then graciously shook the hands of Chris, Spooney and Texas Eddie. "I don't quite know what words to use to properly say just how much I appreciate what you gentlemen did for me, thank you so very much. I was very foolish and gullible, but now I'm much wiser. This money is for a down payment on our dear mother's dream home. She has not accepted the lifestyle here in Vegas so we decided to take her back home to Maryland where we know she will be content and happy."

They spent the balance of the morning talking over the times they had back east and the hours slipped by quickly. An hour before flight time they all piled into Joshau's van and drove to the airport. Once there the two brothers said their goodbyes and promised to look them up when they return to Maryland.

After checking in at the airline counter they headed for the restaurant to kill the fifteen minutes they had left before taking off. As they were sipping their coffee, Chris suddenly placed his cup on the table and lowered his head in an effort to hide his face. Spooney noticed this immediately and asked him if he was alright. At first he thought

Chris may have spotted Bart and Nemo. Chris whispered, "Do you guys remember the dude that I dumped somewhere in Maryland so he wouldn't show up at the Glen Rock game?"

"Yeah," replied Spooney, "His name was John something or other from Denver."

"John Bourne is his name and he just walked in the door. He might not recognize me since I wore a wig, mustache and glasses when I picked him up at BWI but he'll most likely recognize you. Let's keep a low profile and maybe he won't notice us."

Bourne sat at the counter near the door where the guys would have to pass right by him to exit the restaurant. He would surely recognize Spooney which meant big trouble, something they didn't need at this stage of their life.

With only minutes to go before boarding their plane they tried to come up with some sort of diversion that would allow them to get by him without being recognized.

Without a word being said, Texas Eddie got up from the table and walked out of the restaurant. The three looked at each other wondering if he left to avoid any forthcoming trouble.

Hearing the call to board their plane they decided to chance it and leave. Suddenly they heard and announcement, "Your attention please, will Mr. John Bourne come to the information desk, there is an urgent message for you."

The three looked at each other and began laughing for they knew that Jonsey came through for them again. Spooney remarked, "Wonder what he's going to charge us for that?"

As quickly as they could, they scampered across the terminal, avoiding the information desk, and immediately boarded their plane where they found Texas Eddie sitting in his assigned seat with his legs crossed and reading a magazine.

Spooney asked him if he really left John Bourne a message.

"Of course I did," he replied.

"What did the message say?"

Texas Eddie pulled a pen from his pocket and wrote something on the back of the magazine he was reading and handed it to Spooney.

He burst into a hardy laugh when the read the word "SUCKER."

The End

CPSIA information can be obtained at www.ICGtesting.com
Printed in the USA
BVOW08s0953130815

413222BV00001B/8/P